Sonnets from the Portuguese XLIII
by Elizabeth Barrett Browning (1806–1861)

How do I love thee? Let me count the ways.
I love thee to the depth and breadth and height
My soul can reach, when feeling out of sight
For the ends of Being and ideal Grace.
I love thee to the level of everyday's
Most quiet need, by sun and candle-light.
I love thee freely, as men strive for Right;
I love thee purely, as they turn from Praise.
I love thee with a passion put to use
In my old griefs, and with my childhood's faith.
I love thee with a love I seemed to lose
With my lost saints,—I love thee with the breath,
Smiles, tears, of all my life!—and, if God choose,
I shall but love thee better after death.

THE ITALIAN'S WIFE
BY SUNSET

Please return on or before the latest date above.
You can renew online at *www.kent.gov.uk/libs*
or by telephone 08458 247 200

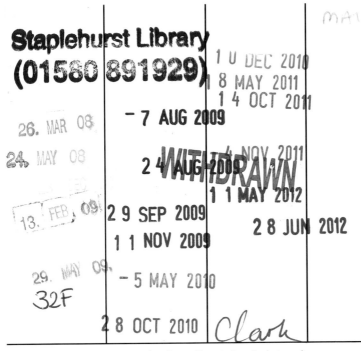

THE ITALIAN'S WIFE BY SUNSET

BY

LUCY GORDON

Pure reading pleasure

First published in Great Britain 2007
Large Print edition 2007
Harlequin Mills & Boon Limited,
Eton House, 18-24 Paradise Road,
Richmond, Surrey TW9 1SR

© Lucy Gordon 2007

ISBN: 978 0 263 19507 1

Set in Times Roman 16½ on 20 pt.
16-1207-47696

Printed and bound in Great Britain
by Antony Rowe Ltd, Chippenham, Wiltshire

CHAPTER ONE

THE picture on the computer screen seemed to fill the room with humour and good cheer. It showed a young man of strikingly attractive looks, fair, shaggy hair, dark blue glowing eyes and a smile that hinted at mischief.

'Oh, wow!' Jackie sighed. 'Just look at him!'

Della chuckled indulgently. Her secretary was young and easily moved by male beauty. She, herself, tried to be more detached.

'He's not bad,' she conceded.

'Not bad?' Jackie echoed, scandalised. 'He's a dream.'

'But I need more than a pretty face. I need a man who really knows his stuff, preferably one who's already made a name for himself.'

'Della, this is a TV series you're producing. It matters how he looks.'

'Yes, it matters that he looks like a serious expert and not a mere boy. Carlo Rinucci can't be more than about twenty-five.'

'According to his data he's thirty,' Jackie said, thumbing through papers. 'And he has a big reputation in ruins and bones and things like that.'

'But he's Italian. I can't have him fronting an English television series.'

'Some of which will be based in Italy. Besides, it says here that he speaks perfect English, and you've said yourself that you have to sell the series internationally if it's to make any money.'

This was true. In the world of television Della was a big shot, with her own production company and a brilliant reputation. Her programmes were in great demand. Even so, she had to consider the practicalities.

She studied Carlo Rinucci's face again, and had to admit that he had a lot going for him. He wasn't merely handsome. His grin had a touch of delightful wickedness, as though he'd discovered a secret hidden from the rest of the world.

'I had an uncle once,' Jackie said. 'He was a

travelling salesman with a girl in every town and a line in flattery that would charm the birds off the trees. And no matter what he did everyone forgave him, just for the sake of his smile. Dad used to say Uncle Joe hadn't just eaten the Apple of Life, he'd gone to live in the tree.'

'And you think he's the same?' Della mused, scrutinising Carlo's laughing face.

'I'd take a bet on it.'

Privately Della agreed, but she kept that thought to herself. Her hard-won caution was warning her not to go overboard for this young man just because he looked good. Very good. Marvellous.

His resumé was certainly impressive. George Franklin, her assistant, who was helping to research this series, had e-mailed her.

Don't be misled by his youth. Carlo Rinucci is the up-and-coming man in his field. He's done some impressive work and written a couple of books that have attracted attention. His opinions are often unorthodox, but his work is sound.

He'd added a few notes about Carlo Rinucci's current project at Pompeii, the little town just south of Naples, buried long ago in the lava of the erupting volcano Vesuvius, and he'd finished with the words: *Believe me, he's worth investigating.*

'Worth investigating,' Della murmured.

'I'll investigate him for you,' Jackie said eagerly. 'I could get the next plane to Naples, look him over and report back.'

'Nice try,' Della said, amused.

'You mean you've already bagged him for yourself?'

'I mean,' Della said severely, 'that I shall consider all the options in a serious and practical way, make my evaluation, and decide what is best for the programme.'

'That's what I said. You've bagged him for yourself.'

Della laughed and dropped her formal tone.

'Well, there has to be some advantage in being the boss,' she said.

'No kidding! If you use him the ratings will go through the roof. Every country will want to buy the programme. You'll have a great reputation.'

'Some people think I already have a reputation,' Della said in mock offence.

'Not like the one you'll have if he's working for you.'

'So you think I should hire him to make my name for me? Thanks a lot, but I don't need help from him or any other pretty boy getting through life on his charm.'

'You don't know that he's char—'

'Just look at the time! You should be going home.'

Jackie departed, but not without one final lingering look at the computer screen.

'Behave yourself,' Della commanded, laughing. 'He's not that gorgeous.'

'Oh, yes, he is,' Jackie sighed as she retreated and closed the door.

For Della there was no journey to and from work, as she ran her business from her own home—a houseboat moored on the Thames, near Chelsea. She treasured it, not only for its own sake, but also as a symbol of the distance she'd travelled since the day she'd started out with almost nothing.

Now that it was six o'clock her working day

hadn't ended, merely moved into a new phase—making calls to the other side of the world in different time zones. She kicked off her shoes and settled down.

Carlo Rinucci's face was still on the screen, but she refused to allow him to distract her. She reached out for the mouse, ready to click him into cyberspace, but her hand paused of its own accord.

Right from the start she'd insisted that the presenter for her series about places of great historical events must be someone with an impressive academic name.

'I don't want a handsome talking head who's going to reveal himself as a dumb cluck the minute he doesn't have a script,' she'd said. 'In fact, I'll expect him to write a lot of the script.'

She'd reviewed a host of possibilities, both male and female, all serious people with impressive reputations. One woman had aroused great hopes, but in the audition she became pompous. One man had seemed a real possibility—in his forties, elegant, serious, yet attractively suave—until he stood in front of a camera and became tongue-tied.

'I'll bet you're never lost for words,' she said,

addressing the screen. 'Just looking at you, I know that. You can talk the hind legs off a donkey, which probably helped you get some of those fine-sounding qualifications.'

Then she stopped and stared. She could have sworn he'd winked at her.

'Enough of that,' she reproved him sternly. 'I know your kind. My second husband was just like you. Talk about charm! The trouble was, charm was all Gerry had—unless you include a genius for spending other people's money.'

She poured herself a drink and leaned back, contemplating the face with reluctant pleasure.

'Am I being unreasonable?' she asked him. 'Am I against you just because other people are for you? I know I'm a bit contrary. At least, folk claim that I am. They say I'm difficult, awkward, stubborn—and that's just my friends talking. But I've got a good life. I have a career that gives me all I want, and I'm immune to male attraction— well, sort of immune. Most of the time. You do nothing for me. Nothing at all.'

But he didn't believe her. She could see that in his face.

She gazed at him. He gazed back. What came next hovered inevitably in the air between them.

'So I guess,' she said slowly, 'there's no reason why I can't set up a meeting and look you over.'

'This place looks as though a bomb had hit it,' Hope Rinucci observed.

She was surveying her home: first the main room, then the dining room, then the terrace overlooking the Bay of Naples with a distant view of Vesuvius.

'Two bombs,' she added, viewing the disarray.

But she did not speak with disapproval, more like satisfaction. The previous evening there had been a party, and in Hope's opinion a party that didn't leave the surroundings looking shattered was no party at all.

By that standard last night had been a triumphant success.

Ruggiero, one of her younger sons, came into the room very carefully, and immediately sat down.

'It was a great night,' he said faintly.

'It was indeed,' she said at once. 'We had so much to celebrate. Francesco's new job. Primo and Olympia, with Olympia's parents over from England, and the news that she's going to have a baby. And then Luke and Minnie saying that they're going to have a baby, too.'

'And then there's Carlo,' Ruggiero mused, naming his twin. 'Mamma, did you ever work out which of those three young ladies was actually his girlfriend?'

'Not exactly,' she said, taking him a black coffee, which he received gratefully. 'They all seemed to arrive together. If only Justin and Evie could have been here as well. But she is so heavily pregnant with the twins that I can understand her not wanting to travel. She promised to bring them to see us as soon as possible after they arrive.'

'So we can have another party,' Ruggiero said. 'Perhaps by then Carlo will have managed to divide himself into three.'

'Do you know which lady he went home with?'

'I didn't see him leave, but I have the impression that they all went together,' Ruggiero said enviously. '*Mio dio*, but he's a brave man!'

'Who's a brave man?' Francesco asked, coming carefully into the room.

Hope smiled and poured another coffee.

'Carlo,' she said. 'He brought three young ladies last night. Didn't you see?'

'He didn't notice anything but that exotic redhead,' Ruggiero said. 'Where did you find her?'

Francesco thought for a minute before saying, 'She found me—I think.'

'We were wondering which of his dates Carlo took home to his apartment,' Ruggiero said.

'He didn't go back there,' Francesco observed.

'How can you possibly know that?' Hope asked.

'Because he's here.'

Francesco pointed to a large sofa facing the window. Leaning over the back, the others saw a young man stretched out, blissfully asleep. He was in the clothes he'd worn the previous night, his shirt open at the throat, revealing smooth, tanned skin. Everything about him radiated sensual contentment.

'Hey!' Ruggiero prodded him rudely.

'Mmm?'

His twin prodded him again, and Carlo's eyes opened.

It was a source of intense irritation to his

brothers that Carlo didn't awake bleary-eyed and vague, like normal people. Even after sleeping off a night of indulgence he was instantly alert, bright-eyed and at his best. As Ruggiero had once remarked, it was enough to make anyone want to commit murder.

'Hallo,' he said, sitting up and yawning.

'What are you doing there?' Ruggiero demanded, incensed.

'What's wrong with my being here? Ah, coffee! Lovely! Thanks, Mamma.'

'Take no notice of this pair,' Hope advised him. 'They're jealous.'

'Three,' Ruggiero mourned. 'He had three, and he slept on the sofa.'

'The trouble is that three is too many,' Carlo said philosophically. 'One is ideal, two is manageable if you're feeling adventurous, but anything more is a just a problem. Besides, I wasn't at my best by the end of the evening, so I played safe, called a taxi for the ladies and went to sleep.'

'I hope you paid their fares in advance,' Hope said.

'Of course I did,' Carlo said, faintly shocked. 'You brought me up properly.'

Francesco was aghast.

'Of all the spineless, feeble—'

'I know, I know.' Carlo sighed. 'I feel very ashamed.'

'And you call yourself a Rinucci?' Ruggiero said.

'That's enough,' Hope reproved them. 'Carlo behaved like a gentleman.'

'He behaved like a wimp,' Francesco growled.

'True,' Carlo agreed. 'But there can be great benefits to being a wimp. It makes the ladies *think* you're a perfect gentleman, and then, when next time comes—'

He drained his coffee, kissed his mother on the cheek, and escaped before his brothers vented their indignation on him.

The Hotel Vallini was the best Naples had to offer. It stood halfway up a hill, looking down on the city, with a superb view across the bay.

Standing on her balcony, Della kept quite still, regarding Vesuvius, where it loomed through the heat haze. There was nowhere in Naples to escape the sight of the great volcano, with its combination of threat and mystery. Its huge eruption nearly two thousand years ago, burying Pompeii in one day, had become such a legend that it was the first site Della had chosen when she was planning her series.

The three-hour flight had left her feeling tired and sticky. It had been a relief to step under a cool shower, wash away the dust, then dress in fresh clothes. The look she'd chosen was neat and unshowy, almost to the point of austerity: black linen pants, and a white blouse whose plainness didn't disguise its expensive cut.

Businesslike, she told herself. Which was true, but only partly. The outfit might have been designed to show off her tall, slim figure, with its small, elegant breasts and neat behind. Just how much satisfaction this gave her was her own secret.

Her face told a subtly different story, the full mouth having a touch of voluptuousness that was at variance with her chic outline. Her rich, light brown hair was sometimes pulled back in severe lines, but today she'd let it fall about her face in gentle curves, emphasising the sensuality of her face.

The contrast between this and the plain way she dressed caused a lot of enjoyable confusion among her male acquaintances. And she didn't mind that at all.

She had told nobody that she was coming, preferring to take her quarry unawares. She didn't even know that Carlo Rinucci would be at Pompeii today, only that he was working on a project that concerned the place, investigating new theories.

She hurried downstairs. It was early afternoon, and just time enough to get out there and form the impressions that would help her when she went into action next day.

Taking a taxi to the railway station, she bought a ticket for the Circumvesuviana, the light railway that ran between Naples and Pompeii, taking about half an hour. For most of that time she sat gazing out of the window at Vesuvius, dominating the landscape, growing ever nearer.

From the station it was a short walk to the Porta Marina, the city gate to Pompeii, where she purchased a ticket and entered the ruined city.

The first thing that struck her was the comparative quiet. Tourists thronged the dead streets, yet their noise did not rise above a gentle murmur, and when she turned aside into an empty yard she found herself almost in silence.

After the bustle of her normal life the peace was delightful. Slowly she turned around, looking at the ancient stones, letting the quiet seep into her.

'Come here! Do you hear me? *Come here at once.*'

The shriek rent the atmosphere, and the next moment she saw why. A boy of about twelve was running through the ruins, hopping nimbly over stones, hotly pursued by a middle-aged woman who was trying to run and shout at the same time.

'Come here!' she called in English.

The youngster made the mistake of looking back, which distracted him enough for Della to step into his path and grab him.

'Lemme go!' he gasped, struggling.

'Sorry, no can do,' she said, friendly but implacable.

'Thank you,' puffed the teacher, catching up.

'Mickey, you stop that. Come back to the rest of the class.'

'But it's boring,' the boy wailed. 'I hate history.'

'We're on a school trip,' the woman explained. 'The chance of a lifetime. I'd have been thrilled to go to Italy when I was at school, but they're all the same, these kids. Ungrateful little so-and-sos!'

'It's boring,' repeated the boy sullenly.

The two women looked at each other sympathetically. Quick as a flash the lad took his chance to dart away again, and managed to get out of sight around a corner. By the time they followed he'd found another corner and vanished again.

'Oh heavens! My class!' wailed the teacher.

'You go back to them while I find him,' Della said.

It was easier said than done. The boy appeared to have vanished into the stones. Della ran from street to street without seeing him.

At last she saw two men standing by a large hole in the ground, evidently considering the contents seriously. The younger man looked as though he'd just been working in the earth. Through his sleeveless vest she could see the glisten of sweat on strong, young muscles, and he was breathing hard.

In desperation she hailed them.

'Did a boy in a red shirt run past? He's a pupil escaping from a school party and his teacher is frantic.'

'I didn't see anyone,' the older man remarked. 'What about you, Carlo?'

Before she could react to the name the young man with his back to her turned, smiling. It was the face she'd come to see, handsome, merry, relaxed.

'I haven't noticed—' he began to say, but broke off to cry, *'There!'*

The boy had appeared through an arch and started running across the street. Carlo Rinucci darted after him, dodging back and forth through archways. The boy's scowl vanished, replaced by a smile. Carlo grinned back, and it soon became a game.

Then the other children appeared, a dozen of them, hurling themselves into the game with delight.

'Oh, dear!' sighed the teacher.

'Leave them to it,' Della advised. 'I'm Della Hadley, by the way.'

'Hilda Preston. I'm supposed to be in charge of that lot. What am I going to do now?'

'I don't think you need to do anything,' Della said, amused. 'He's doing it all.'

It was true. The youngsters had crowded around the young man, and by some mysterious magic he had calmed them down, and was now leading them back to the teacher.

Like the Pied Piper, Della thought, considering him with her head on one side.

'OK, that's enough,' he said, approaching. 'Cool it, kids.'

'Whatever do you think you're doing?' Hilda demanded of the youngsters. 'You know I told you to stay close to me.'

'But it's boring,' complained the boy who'd made a run for it.

'I don't care if it is,' she snapped, goaded into honesty. 'I've brought you here to get some culture, and that's what you're going to get.'

Della heard a soft choke nearby, and turned to see Carlo fighting back laughter. Since she was doing the same herself, a moment of perfect understanding flashed between them. They both put their hands over their mouths at the same moment.

Predictably, the word *culture* had caused the pupils to emit groans of dismay. Some howled to heaven, others clutched their stomachs. One joker even rolled on the ground.

'Now she's done it,' Carlo muttered to Della. 'The forbidden word—one that should never be spoken, save in a terrified whisper. And she said it out loud.'

'What word is that?'

He looked wildly around, to be sure nobody was listening, before saying in a ghostly voice, 'Culture.'

'Oh, yes, I see.' She nodded knowingly.

'You'd think a modern schoolteacher would know better. Does she do that often?'

'I don't know—I'm not—' she began, realising that he thought she was one of the school party.

'Never mind,' he said. 'It's time for a rescue operation.' Raising his voice, he said, 'You can all calm down, because this place has nothing to do with culture. This place is about people dying.' For good measure he added, *'Horribly!'*

Hilda was aghast. 'He mustn't say things like that. They're just children.'

'Children love gore and horror,' Della pointed out.

'It's about nightmares,' Carlo went on, 'and the greatest catastrophe the world has ever known. Thousands of people, living their ordinary lives, when there was an ominous rumble in the distance and Vesuvius erupted, engulfing the town. People died in the middle of fights, of meals—thousands of them, frozen in one place for nearly two thousand years.'

He had them now. Everyone was listening.

'Is it true they've got the dead bodies in the museum?' someone asked, with relish.

'Not the actual bodies,' Carlo said, in the tone of a man making a reluctant admission, and there was a groan of disappointment.

Bloodthirsty little tykes, Della thought, amused. But he's right about them.

'They were trapped and died in the lava,' Carlo continued, 'and when they were excavated, centuries later, the bodies had perished, leaving holes in the lava of the exact shapes. So the bodies could be reconstructed in plaster.'

'And can we see them?'

'Yes, you can see them.'

A sigh of blissful content showed that his audience was with him. He began to expand on the subject, making it vibrantly alive. He spoke fluently, in barely accented English, with an actor's sense of the dramatic. Suddenly the streets were populated with heroes and villains, beautiful heroines, going about their daily business, then running hopelessly for their lives.

Della seized the chance to study him in action. It went against the grain to give him top marks, but she had to admit that he ticked every box. The looks she'd admired on the screen were enhanced by the fact that his hair needed a trim, and hung in shaggy curls about his face.

He looked like Jack the Lad—a brawny roustabout without a thought in his head beyond the next beer, the next girl, or the next night spent living it up. What he didn't look like was an academic with a swathe of degrees, one of them in philosophy.

'History isn't about culture,' he finally reassured them. 'It's about people living and dying, loving and hating—just like us. Now, go with your teachers and behave yourself, or I'll drown you in lava.'

A cheer showed that this threat was much appreciated.

'Thank you,' Hilda said. 'You really do have a gift with children.'

He grinned, his teeth gleaming against the light tan of his face.

'I'm just a born show-off,' he laughed.

That was true, Della mused. In fact, he was exactly what she needed.

Hilda thanked her and turned to shepherd the children away. Carlo looked at her in surprise.

'Aren't you with them?' he asked.

'No, I just happened along,' she said.

'And found yourself in the middle of it, huh?'

They both laughed.

'That poor woman,' Della said. 'Whoever sent her here on a culture trip should have known better.'

He put out his hand.

'My name is Carlo Rinucci.'

'Yes, I—' She was about to say that she knew who he was, but hastily changed it to, 'I'm Della Hadley.'

'It is a great pleasure to meet you, *signorina*— or should that be *signora*?'

'Technically, yes. I'm divorced.'

He gave her a gentle, disarming smile, still holding her hand.

'I'm so glad,' he said.

Watch it, warned a voice in her head. He plays this game too well.

'Hey, Carlo,' called the other man, 'are you going to give the *signora* her hand back, or shall we put it in the museum with the others?'

She snatched her hand back, suddenly self-conscious. Carlo, she noticed, wasn't self-conscious at all. He just gave a grin that he clearly knew would always win him goodwill.

'I forgot about Antonio,' he admitted.

'Don't mind me,' Antonio said genially. 'I've just been doing the work while you do your party tricks.'

'Why don't we finish for the day?' Carlo said. 'Time's getting on, and Signora Hadley wants a coffee.'

'Yes, I want one desperately,' she said, discovering it to be true.

'Then let's go.' He looked her in the eye and said significantly, 'We've lost too much time already.'

CHAPTER TWO

DELLA waited while he showered at top speed, then emerged casually dressed in a white short-sleeved shirt and fawn trousers. Even in this simple attire he looked as though he could afford the world, and she guessed that he'd had a privileged upbringing.

'Let's get that coffee,' Carlo said.

But when they reached the self-service cafeteria they both stopped dead. The place was packed with tourists, all yelling with raucous good cheer.

'I think not,' he said firmly.

He didn't wait for her answer, but simply took her hand and walked away, adding, 'I know lots of better places.'

But then, abruptly, he stopped.

'Where are my manners?' he demanded, striking himself on the forehead. 'I didn't ask if you wanted to go into that place. Shall we turn back?'

'Don't you dare,' she said at once.

He grinned, nodding, and they went on in perfect accord.

His car was just what she would have expected—an elegant sports two-seater in dashing red—and, also as she would have expected, he ushered her into it with a flourish. His whole body was a clever combination of different effects. Built like a hunk, yet he moved with subtlety and grace. His hands on the steering wheel held her attention, lying there lightly, barely touching, yet controlling the powerful machine effortlessly.

Della's mind was reeling.

Just what I need, she thought. He's ideal—for the programme. Handsome, charming, never at a loss for words—*he* won't suddenly become tongue-tied in front of a camera, or anywhere else. The perfect— She paused in her thoughts and tried to remember that she was a television producer. 'The perfect *product*. Yes, that's it.

She felt better once she'd settled that with herself.

'Do you live around here?' Carlo asked.

'No, I'm just visiting. I'm staying at the Vallini in Naples.'

'Are you planning to stay long?'

'I—haven't quite decided,' she said carefully.

He swung onto the coast road and they drove with the sea on their left, glittering in the late-afternoon sun. Naples lay ahead, but when they reached halfway he turned off into a tiny seaside village. Della could see fishing boats tied up at the water's edge, and cobbled streets stretching away between old houses.

He parked the car and made his way confidently to a small restaurant. As soon as they entered a man behind the counter yelled joyfully, *'E, Carlo!'*

'Berto!' he yelled back cheerfully, and guided Della to a table by a small window.

Berto came hurrying over with coffee, which he contrived to pour while chattering and giving Della quick, appraising glances.

I'll bet they see him in here with a new companion every week, she thought, with an inner chuckle.

The coffee was delicious, and she began to relax for the first time since she'd awoken that morning.

'It was so good to get off that plane,' she said, giving herself a little shake.

'You just arrived from England?'

'You could tell because I'm speaking English, right?'

'It's a bit more than that. My mother is English, and there's something in your voice that sounds a little like her.'

'That explains a lot about you, too.'

'Such as what?' he asked curiously.

'You speak English with barely an accent.'

He laughed. 'That was Mamma's doing. We all had to speak her language perfectly, or else.'

'All? You have plenty of brothers and sisters?'

'Just brothers. There are six of us, related in various ways.'

'Various?' She frowned. 'I thought you just said you were brothers.'

'Some of us are brothers, some of us are "sort of" brothers. When Mamma married Poppa she already had two sons, plus a stepson and an adopted son. Then they had two more.'

'Six Rinucci brothers?' she mused.

'It doesn't bear thinking about, does it?' he said solemnly. 'It's just terrible.'

His droll manner made her chuckle, and he went

on, 'Even the most Italian of us are part English, but some are more English than others. The differences get blurred. Poppa says we're all the devil's spawn anyway, so what does it matter?'

'It sounds like a lovely, big, happy family.' She sighed enviously.

'I suppose it is,' he said, seeming to consider. 'We fight a lot, but we always make up.'

'And you'd always be there for each other. That's the nicest thing.'

'You said that like an only child,' he observed, regarding her with interest.

'Is it that obvious?' she asked.

'It is to someone who has many siblings.'

'I must admit that I really envy you that,' she said. 'Tell me some more about your brothers. You don't fight all the time, surely?'

'On and off. Mamma's first husband was English, but his first wife had been Italian—a Rinucci. Primo is the son of that marriage, so he's half-Italian, half-English. Luke, the adopted son of that marriage is all English. Are you with me?'

'Struggling, but still there. Keep going.'

'Primo and Luke have always traded insults,

but that means nothing. It's practically a way of communicating—especially while they were in love with the same woman.'

'Ouch!'

'Luckily that didn't last very long. Primo married her, and Luke found someone else, and now their wives keep them in order, just as wives should.'

'Oh, really?' she said ironically.

'No, really. Any man who's grown up in this country knows that when the wife speaks the husband stands to attention—if he's wise. Well, it's what my father does, anyway.'

'And when your turn comes you'll choose a woman who knows how to keep you in order?'

'No, my mother will choose her,' he assured her solemnly. 'She's set her heart on six daughters-in-law, and so far she's only achieved three. Every time a new woman enters the house I'll swear she checks her for suitability and ticks off a list. When she finds the right one I'll get my orders.'

'And you'll obey?' she teased.

His answering grin was rich with life, an invitation to join him in adventure.

'That's a while off yet,' he said contentedly. 'I'm in no rush.'

'Life's good, so why spoil it with a wife?'

'I wouldn't exactly put it like that,' he said uneasily.

'Yes, you would,' she said at once. 'Not out loud, perhaps. But deep inside, where you think I can't hear.'

His answer was unexpected.

'I wouldn't bet against your being able to hear anything I was thinking.'

Then he looked disconcerted, as though he had surprised even himself with the words, and his laugh had a touch of awkwardness that affected her strangely.

Berto came to their table to tell them that the day's catch of clams was excellent, and that *spaghetti alle vongole* could be rustled up in a moment.

'Clam pasta,' Carlo translated.

'Sounds lovely.'

'Wine?' Berto queried.

Carlo eyed her questioningly, and she hastened to say, 'I leave everything to you.'

He rattled off several names that Della didn't recognise, and Berto bustled away.

'I took the liberty of ordering a few other things as well,' Carlo explained.

'That's fine. I wouldn't have known what to ask for.'

His eyes gleamed. 'Playing the tactful card, huh?'

'I'm a newcomer here. I listen to the expert.'

Berto returned with white wine. When he had poured it and gone, Carlo said, 'So, you reckon you can see right through me?'

'No, *you* said I could. Not me.'

'I have to admit that you got one or two things right.'

'Let's see how well I manage on the rest. I know Italian men often stay at home longer than others, but I don't think that you do, because Mamma's eagle eye might prove—shall we say, inhibiting?'

'That's as good a word as any,' he conceded cautiously.

'You've got a handy little bachelor apartment where you take the girls you can't take home because they wouldn't tick any of Mamma's "suitability" boxes, and that's just fine by you—'

'*Basta!*' He stopped her with a pleading voice. 'Enough, enough! How did you learn all that?'

'Easy. I just took one look at you.'

'Obviously I don't have any secrets,' he said ruefully.

'Well, perhaps I was a little unfair on you.'

'No, you weren't. I deserved it all. In fact, I'm worse. My mother would certainly say so.'

She chuckled. 'Then think of me as a second mother.'

'Not in a million years,' he said softly.

His eyes, gliding significantly over her, made his meaning plain beyond words, and suddenly she was aware that she looked several years younger than her age, that her figure was ultra-slim and firm, thanks to hours in the gym, that her eyes were large and lustrous and her complexion flawless.

Every detail of her body might have been designed to elicit a man's admiration. She knew it, and at this moment she was passionately glad of it.

It might be fun.

He was certainly fun.

Berto arrived with clam pasta, breaking the mood—which was a relief, since she hadn't decided where she wanted this to go. But a moment ago there had been no choice to make. What had happened?

He was watching her face as she ate, relishing her enjoyment.

'Good?'

'Good,' she confirmed. 'I love Italian food, but I don't get much chance to eat it.'

'You've never been here before?'

'I had a holiday in Italy once, but mostly I depend on Italian restaurants near my home.'

'Where do you live?'

'In London, on a houseboat moored on the Thames.'

'You live on the water? That's great. Tell me about it.'

At this point she should have talked about her serious day-to-day life, with its emphasis on work, and the occasional visit from her grown up son. Instead, unaccountably, Della found herself describing the river at dawn, when the first light caught the ripples and the banks emerged from the shadows.

'Sometimes it feels really strange,' she mused. 'I'm right there, in the heart of a great city, yet it's so quiet on the river just before everywhere comes alive. It's as though the world belongs to me alone, just for a little while. But you have to catch the moment because it vanishes so quickly. The light grows and the magic dies.'

'I know what you mean,' he murmured.

'You've been there?'

'No, I—I meant something else. Later. Tell me some more about yourself. What sort of work do you do?'

'I'm in television,' she said vaguely.

'You're a star—your face on every screen?'

'No, I'm strictly behind the scenes.'

'Ah, you're one of those terrifyingly efficient production assistants who gets everyone scurrying about.'

'I've been told I can be terrifying,' she admitted. 'And people have been known to scurry around when I want them to.'

'Maybe that's why I thought you were a schoolteacher?'

'You've got quite a way with youngsters yourself.'

But he dismissed the suggestion with a gesture of his hand.

'I'd be a terrible teacher. I could never keep discipline. They'd all see through me and know that I was just one of the kids at heart.'

'You had them hanging on your every word.'

'That's because I'm crazy about my subject and I want everyone else to be crazy, too. I believe it can make me a bit of a bore.'

'Sure, I'm sitting here fainting with boredom. Tell me about your subject.'

'Archaeology. No, don't say it—' He interrupted himself quickly. 'I don't look like an archaeologist, more like a hippie—'

'I was thinking a hobo myself,' she said mischievously. 'Someone not very respectable, anyway.'

'Thank you. I take that as a compliment. I'm not respectable. I don't pretend to be. Who needs it?'

'Nobody, as long as you know your stuff— and you obviously do.'

Carlo grinned. 'Why? Because I kept a few youngsters quiet? That's the easy part, being a showman. It's not what really counts.'

She'd actually been thinking of his string of qualifications, but remembered in time that she wasn't supposed to know about them.

'What does really count?' she asked, fascinated.

That was all he needed. Words poured from him. Some she understood, some were above her head, but what was crystal-clear was his devotion, amounting to a love affair, to ancient times and other worlds.

All his life he'd had soaring ambitions, hating the thought of being earthbound.

'I used to play truant at school,' he recalled, 'and my teachers all predicted I'd come to a bad end because I was bound to fail my exams. But I fooled 'em. I used to sit up the night before, memorising everything just long enough to pass with honours.' He sighed with happy recollection. 'Lord, but that made them mad!'

She couldn't help laughing at the sight of him, transformed back into that rebellious schoolboy.

'I couldn't face anything nine-to-five,' he said.

'Not at school, not at work. The beauty of being in my line is that you get to fly.'

'And you really have to fly,' she teased. 'I guess when you get near the earth you crash.'

'Right. That's why I could never be a teacher, or a museum administrator. I might have to—' He looked desperate.

'Might have to what?' she asked through her laughter.

He glanced over his shoulder and spoke with a lowered voice.

'Wear a collar and tie.'

He sat back with the air of one who had described unimaginable horrors. Della nodded in sympathy.

'But doesn't it ever get depressing?' she asked. 'Spending so much time surrounded by death, especially in Pompeii—all those people, petrified in the positions they died in nearly two thousand years ago?'

'But they're not dead,' he said, almost fiercely. 'Not to me. They're still speaking, and I'm listening because they have so much to say.'

'But hasn't it all been said? I mean, they

finished excavating that place years ago. What more is there?'

He almost tore his hair.

'They didn't finish excavating. They barely started. I'm working on a whole undiscovered area—'

He stopped, and seemed to calm himself down by force of will.

'I'm sorry. Once I get started there's no stopping me. I told you I'm a bore.'

'I wasn't bored,' she said truthfully. 'Not a bit.'

In truth, she was fascinated. A fire was flaming within him and she wanted to see more, know more.

'Go on,' she urged.

Then he was away again, words pouring out in a vivid, passionate stream so that she caught the sense even of the bits she didn't understand. After a while she stopped trying to follow too closely. It didn't matter. What mattered was that he could make her see visions through his own eyes. It was like being taken on a journey into the heart of the man, and it was exhilarating.

'You've let your food get cold,' he said at last.

At some point they had passed onto the next course, and it had lain uneaten on both their plates while he took her on a journey to the stars.

'I forgot about it,' she said, feeling slightly stunned.

'So did I,' he admitted.

The voice of caution, which normally ruled her life, whispered, *A practised charmer,* but the warning floated away, unheeded. Something more was happening—something that would make her get up and leave now, if she had any sense.

But she didn't want to be sensible. She wanted to go on enjoying this foolish magic, as crazy as a teenager. No matter how it ended. She would relish every moment.

Carlo watched her without seeming to. It was becoming important to him to 'capture' her in his mind, as though by doing so he could fit her into some niche where he would know what to make of her. Luckily the hours stretched ahead, full of time to get to know her better.

Then, out of the corner of his eye, Carlo saw an acquaintance come into the restaurant, and he cursed silently. The man was well-meaning but long-winded, and if he didn't act fast his evening would be in ruins.

'I'll be back in a moment,' he said hurriedly, leaving the table.

His worst fears were fulfilled. His friend greeted him with bonhomie, and a determination to join him at all costs. Carlo just managed to head him off at the pass, and finally made his way back to the table, determined on escape.

Della was talking on her cellphone as he approached, and he heard her say, 'It's lovely to talk to you, darling.'

It wasn't so much the word that troubled him as the soft adoration in her voice, the glow in her eyes.

For pity's sake, he chided himself. You've only known her a few hours. What do you care who she calls darling?

He wished he knew the answer.

She was laughing, her face alight with affection.

'I've got to go now. I'll call you again soon. Bye, darling.' She hung up.

A moment later Carlo reached the table, showing no sign that he'd heard the call or even knew she'd made one.

'Perhaps we should move on?' he said.

She nodded. She had seen him talking urgently with a man, blocking his way so that he could not disturb them.

Outside, he took her hand and headed for the car, but then stopped suddenly, as though something had struck him.

'No—wait! The time's just right.'

'Right for what?'

'I'll show you.'

He turned and began to lead her in the opposite direction. Gradually the houses fell away and they were going towards the shore, reaching the road that ran beside it and crossing over onto the beach.

'Look,' he said.

The tide had gone out, leaving the fishing boats lying lop-sided on the wet sand. Water lay in the ridges and the tiny pools, and the last rays of the setting sun had turned it deep red.

She gazed, awestruck, at so much dramatic beauty before finally breathing, 'It's magic.'

'Yes, it is. Not everyone sees it, but I thought you would because of what you told me about dawn on the Thames. To some people it's just wet sand and a few boats. If you see them by day they're old and shabby. But like this—'

He stopped, almost as if hoping that she would finish his thought.

'Another world,' she said. 'A special world that only appears for a short time.'

She thought he gave a little sigh of pleasure.

'Just a short time,' he agreed. 'Soon it will be dark, and the special world will vanish.'

'But it'll return tomorrow.'

'It may not. It isn't always like this, only when everything is right. It's like you said: you have to be ready to catch the moment before it vanishes.'

He was leading her out in the direction of the sea, leaving the conventional safety of the land behind, taking her into an unfamiliar world.

'Wait,' she said. 'Let me take off my shoes before they get wet.'

She did so, shoving them into her capacious shoulder bag. He removed his own and she grabbed them, putting them, too, into the bag, and taking his hand again.

Not speaking, they walked towards the horizon, until the shallow water just covered their feet.

'This is when it's at its best,' he said quietly.

The setting sun covered the beach and the film of water with blazing red in all directions, so that they might have been standing in a fire. It drenched them with its mysterious violent light.

Carlo looked at her, smiling, and she braced herself, knowing that this was exactly the right moment for a skilled charmer to kiss her, and that he, who clearly knew all the moves, would be bound to make this one. But then she saw that there was something awkward, almost shy, about his smile. While she was trying to puzzle it out, he raised her hand and rubbed the back of it against his cheek.

She stared, too dumbfounded to react. According to the script he should have kissed her, and if he'd done so she would have known how to 'place' him. But the closest he came was to press his lips gently where his cheek had touched a moment earlier. And when she met his eyes she saw that he was as disconcerted as she.

The next moment the light changed. Something brilliant faded. And it was over.

'It's gone,' she said, disappointed.

'It's gone for now,' he agreed. 'But there are other things. Let's go.'

As twilight fell Carlo drove along the coast until they reached the outskirts of Naples.

'Shall I take you to your hotel?' he asked.

'Yes, please. I need to talk to you where we won't be disturbed.'

She knew she couldn't put the moment off any longer. Something had started to happen, and if it were to flower she must be honest with him first.

As they went up in the elevator at the Vallini she was planning how she would explain that their meeting had not been an accident. Such was his good nature that she had no fears about his reaction.

The last of the light faded as they entered her room and shut the door. Before she could reach for the switch she felt his arms go around her, drawing her close, fitting her head against his shoulder.

At once she relaxed. This was what she'd wanted for at least the last hour. Why deny it? It was undignified to have fallen so easily into the trap, especially as she had seen it from a distance, but that was what had happened.

But the trap wasn't the one she'd armed herself against. A glib tongue and an easy manner—those she could cope with. But the uncertainty in his eyes when they'd met hers had caught her unawares

It was the worst moment for her cellphone to buzz. Groaning, Carlo released her, and she turned away, walking to the window as she reached into her purse. Taking out the phone, she discovered a text message.

'Shall we have champagne?' came Carlo's voice from behind her.

She hadn't realised that he was so close, and jumped sharply enough to drop the phone.

'Sorry,' he said. 'I'll get it for you. It went under that chair.'

He dropped to his knees and reached for it. Then, as he drew it out, Della saw his smile fade.

In silence he handed it to her. Her blood ran cold as she saw the words on the illuminated screen.

Have you tracked Rinucci down yet? George

Looking up, she saw Carlo standing back, regarding her. On the surface his good humour seemed unruffled, but she could see the distance in his eyes.

'You came to "track me down"?' he asked coolly.

She sighed. 'Yes, I did come here looking for you.'

'What did I do to merit that?'

'If you'd let me explain in my own way—'

'Just tell me.' His voice was ominously quiet.

'You're ideal for a television show I'm planning. I've got my own production company, and I'm setting up a series about places of great dramatic events in history. I need a frontman, and someone told me you'd be ideal.'

'So you came down to audition me?'

'Not exactly that,' she said uneasily.

'How would you describe it?'

'I wanted to meet you, and—and—'

'And get me to jump through some hoops to see if I was up to your standard? And I obliged, didn't I? I jumped through them all, and then some!'

'Carlo, please—all right, I should have told you before.'

'You sure as hell should.'

'But I couldn't predict what was going to happen. When I saw you with those kids, you were so perfect for my purpose that I couldn't believe my luck—'

'Perfect for your purpose?' he echoed, in a soft, angry voice. 'Yes, it's all been about your purpose, hasn't it? You pulled the strings and I danced.'

'Is it so terrible that I wanted to consider you for a job?'

'Not at all, if you'd been up-front. It's the thought of you peering at me from behind a mask that I can't stand. All the time we've been together I thought—well, never mind what I thought. Just tell me this. Did you plan every single detail?'

'Of course not. How could I? You know that things happened that nobody could have planned.'

'Do I? I'm not sure what I understand any

more. I know that you've been clever—subtle enough for an Italian. I congratulate you. It was a masterly performance.'

'It wasn't all a performance,' she said swiftly.

'You know, I think I'd rather believe that it was. It makes things simpler. I was a fool, but at least I found out before any real harm was done.'

'Carlo, please—if you'd just listen to me—'

'I've done enough of that,' he said, in a deceptively affable tone. 'Let's call it a day. You'd better text George back and tell him that you tracked me down and I said to hell with you. Goodbye.'

He was gone, closing the door behind him.

She wanted to scream with frustration and hurl the phone against the door. Instead she turned out the light and went onto the balcony. From there she could see Carlo's car, parked in front of the hotel, then Carlo himself, hurtling out of the front door and leaping into the driver's seat.

She drew back in case he looked up and saw her, but he only sat for a long moment, hunched behind the wheel, brooding. When at last he roused himself, it was to give the wheel a sharp thump that made the horn blast. After his ironic restraint the sudden spurt of temper was startling.

Then he fired the engine, swung out of the forecourt and vanished down the road. He hadn't once looked up at Della's window.

CHAPTER THREE

AT SEVENTEEN she might have wept into her pillow.
At thirty-seven she lay staring into the darkness,
sad but composed, before finally nodding off.

She even managed a prosaic, unromantic
night's sleep. But next morning Della awoke
early and the memories came flooding back,
bringing regretful thoughts.

It would have been nice, she thought. We could
have been fond of each other for a while, before
he found someone his own age. But, oh boy, did
I ever make a mess of it! If there were a prize for
handling things as badly as possible, I'd win the
gold. I should have known better than to hide the
truth, but I wasn't thinking straight.

At this point she found herself smiling wistfully.

But had any woman ever thought straight in his
company? She doubted it. Not guilty on the

grounds of impaired judgment. She'd wanted to make the moment last, and she had never thought how it would seem to him.

What now? Return to Pompeii and try to find him? After all, he's ideal for the programme.

Nuts to that! She just wanted an excuse to see him again. He was like a light coming on and then going out too soon. But what was done was done. She'd just chalk it up to experience and leave Naples today.

It was a relief to have made up her mind. Jumping out of bed, she stripped and headed for the shower, running it very cold to infuse herself with common sense. She was just drying off when there was a knock on the door.

'Who is it?'

'Room Service.'

She hadn't ordered anything, but perhaps this was courtesy of the hotel. Huddling on a silk dressing gown, she opened the door.

Outside stood a tall man, dressed as a waiter. That was all she could tell, as he was holding the tray high, balanced on the fingers of one hand, at just the right angle to conceal his face.

'*Scusi, signora.*'

He seemed to glide into the room, contriving to keep his features hidden as he headed for the little table by the window and set down the tray.

Della's heart began to dance. He might hide his face, but his hair was unmistakable. Instinctively she pulled together the edges of her thin dressing gown, conscious of how inadequately the silk covered her.

'Orange juice,' he said, turning to her with a flourish. 'Fruit? Cereal?'

'So you're not still angry with me?' she asked, laughing.

'No, I got over my sulk fairly quickly. Forgive me?'

It was so good to see Carlo standing there that she forgot everything else and opened her arms to him. He took two swift steps across the room, and the next moment she was enfolded in an embrace that threatened to crush the breath out of her.

'I was afraid you'd have packed your bags and left last night,' he said between kisses.

'I was afraid I'd never see you again. I'm

sorry. I never meant it to happen the way it did—it just sort of—'

'It doesn't matter. It was my fault for making a fuss about nothing.'

'I always meant to tell you, but things just happened, and I lost track of what I was supposed to be thinking—'

'Yes,' he said with meaning. 'Me too.'

He kissed her again before she could speak, moving his mouth hungrily over hers, pressing her body close against his own. Now she could feel everything she had suspected yesterday, the hard, lean length of him, muscular, sensuously graceful, thrilling.

But it was dangerous to hold him like this when she was nearly naked. The gossamer delicacy of her gown was no protection against the excitement she could sense in him, nor against her own excitement, rising equally fast. Nearly naked wasn't enough. Only complete nakedness would do, for herself and him.

There was an increasingly urgent sense of purpose in the movements of his hands, and her answering desire threatened to overwhelm her. She wanted this. She wanted *him*.

It was the very power of that wanting that made her take fright. Twenty-four hours ago she hadn't met this man. Now she was indulging fantasies of fierce passion, desire with no limits. She must stop this now. She forced herself to tense against him, drawing her head back a little so that he could see her shake it from side to side.

'No—Carlo—please—'

'Della—' His voice was edgy, and it seemed as though he couldn't stop.

'Please—wait—'

She felt his body trembling against hers with the effort of his own restraint, and at last he was still. Now he would think her a tease. But when she looked into his eyes she saw only understanding.

'You're right,' he whispered.

'It's just that—'

'I know—I know—not—not yet.'

He spoke raggedly, but he was in command of himself. Della only wished she could say the same about her own body, which was raging out of control, defying her wise words. She pulled herself free, grabbed some clothes, and vanished into the bathroom.

When she emerged, safely dressed, he had discarded his waiter's jacket and was sitting at the table by the window, pouring her coffee. He seemed calm, with no sign of his recent agitation—except that she thought his hand shook a little.

'Here's food,' he said, indicating rolls and honey. 'But if you need something more substantial I'll buy you a big lunch after we've been to Pompeii.'

'We're going back there?'

'Just for an hour, while I give my team their instructions. Then we'll have the rest of the day free.'

His manner was demure while he served her, as if their moment of blazing physical awareness had never been. But then she glanced up to find him watching her, and it was there in his eyes, memory and, more than that, an anticipation amounting to certainty.

'I'm sorry for what happened,' she said again. 'I was going to tell you last night, but—' She made a helpless gesture.

'It was mostly my fault,' he said, shaking his head. 'I just talked about myself all the time, which is a fault of mine. Mamma always says if I'd shut up now and then I might learn something.'

'But you've never taken her advice long enough to find out if she's right,' Della chuckled.

He grinned. 'You really do sound just like her. Besides, I know now that she *was* right. Today you're going to do all the talking, and I won't say a single word.'

'Hmm!' she said sceptically.

He looked alarmed. 'You understand me too well.'

'In that case we have nothing left to say to each other.'

'Why?'

'Well, isn't that every man's nightmare? A woman who understands him?'

'I'm getting more scared of you every minute.'

'Then you'd better steer well clear of me. If I call the airport now there's bound to be a plane back to London today.'

At once his hand closed over hers, imprisoning it gently but firmly.

'I never run away from danger,' he said lightly. 'How about you?'

There was a moment's hesitation, because something told her that never in her life had she met a danger like this. Then, 'Me neither,' she said.

'Good. In that case…' He paused significantly.

'In that case—?'

'In that case I suggest we hurry up and finish our breakfast.'

She choked into her coffee. She had always been a sucker for a man who could make her laugh.

At Pompeii, his team was waiting for him in the canteen. A brief time in his company had made her more sharply aware of things she had overlooked before, and now she saw at once how the young women in the group brightened as soon as he appeared, and flashed him their best smiles.

She couldn't blame them. There was a life-enhancing quality to him that brought the sun out, and made it natural to smile.

Della lingered only a short while as he talked to them in Italian, which she couldn't understand, then wandered away to the museum.

Here she found what she was looking for—the

plaster casts of the bodies that had lain trapped in their last positions for nearly two thousand years. There was a man who'd fallen on the stairs and never risen again, and another man who'd known the end was coming and curled up in resignation, waiting for the ash to engulf him. Further on, a mother tried vainly to shelter her children.

But it was the lovers who held her the longest. After so many centuries it was still heartbreaking to see the man and woman, stretching out in a vain attempt to reach each other before death swamped them.

'There's such a little distance between their hands,' she murmured.

'Yes, they nearly managed it,' said Carlo beside her.

She didn't know how long he'd been there, and wondered if he'd been watching as she wandered among the 'bodies'.

'And now they'll never reach each other,' she said. 'Trapped for ever with a might-have-been.'

'There's nothing sadder than what might have been,' he agreed. 'That's why I prefer these.'

He led her to another glass case where there

were two forms, a man and a woman, nestled against each other.

'They knew death was coming,' Carlo said, 'but as long as they could meet it in each other's arms they weren't afraid.'

'Maybe,' she said slowly.

'You don't believe that?'

'I wonder if you're stretching imagination too far. You can't really know that they weren't afraid.'

'Can't I? Look at them.'

Della drew nearer and studied the two figures. Their faces were blurred, but she could see that all their attention was for each other, not the oncoming lava. And their bodies were mysteriously relaxed, almost contented.

'You're right,' she said softly. 'While they had each other there was nothing to fear—not even death.'

How would it feel to be like that? she wondered. Two marriages had left her ignorant of that all-or-nothing feeling. What she had known of men had left her cautious, and suddenly it occurred to her that she was deprived.

'Are you ready to go?' he asked.

He drove back to the little fishing village where they had eaten the day before. Now the tide was in, the boats were out, and the atmosphere was completely different. This was another world from that sleepy somnolence, as he proved by taking her to the market, where the stalls were brightly coloured and mostly sold an array of fresh meat and vegetables.

The ones that didn't offered a dazzling variety of handmade silk.

'The area is known for it,' Carlo explained. 'And it's better than anything you'll find in the fashionable shops in Milan.'

As he spoke he was holding up scarves and blouses against her.

'Not these,' he said, tossing a couple aside. 'Not your colour.'

'Isn't it?' she asked, slightly nettled. She had liked both of them.

'No, this is better.' He held up a blouse with a dark blue mottled pattern and considered it against her. 'This one,' he told the woman running the stall.

'Hey, let me check the size,' Della protested.

'No need,' the woman chuckled. 'He always gets the size right.'

'Thank you,' Carlo said hastily, handing over cash and hurrying her away.

'You've got a nerve, buying me clothes without so much as a by-your-leave,' she said.

'You don't have to thank me.'

'I wasn't. I was saying you're as cheeky as a load of monkeys.'

'Slander. All slander.'

To Della's mischievous delight he had definitely reddened.

'So you always get the size right, just by looking?' she mused. 'I mean, always as in *always*?'

'Let's have something to eat,' he said hastily, taking her arm and steering her into a side street where they found a small café.

There he settled her with coffee and a glass of *prosecco*, the white sparkling wine, so light as to be almost a cordial, that Italians loved to drink.

'So now,' he said, 'do what I wouldn't let you do yesterday, and tell me all about yourself. I know you've been married—'

'I married when I was sixteen—and pregnant. Neither of us was old enough to know what we were doing, and when he fled in the first few months I guess I couldn't blame him.'

'I blame him,' he said at once. 'If you do something, you take responsibility for it.'

'Oh, you sound so very old and wise, but how "responsible" were you at seventeen?'

'Perhaps we'd better not go into that,' he said, grinning. 'But he shouldn't have simply have walked out and left you with a baby.'

'Don't feel sorry for me. I wasn't abandoned in a one-room hovel without a penny. We were living with my parents, so I had a comfortable home and someone to take care of me. In fact, I don't think my parents were sorry to see the back of him.'

'Did they give him a nudge?

'He says they did. I'll never really know, but I'm sure it would have happened anyway. It's all for the best. I wouldn't want to be married to the man he is now.'

'Still irresponsible?'

'Worse. Dull.'

'Heaven help us! So you're still in touch?'

'He lives in Scotland. Sol—that's Solomon, our son—visits him. He's there now.'

Light dawned.

'Was Sol the one you were talking to on the phone last night?'

'That's right.'

So there was no other man in her life, he thought, making urgent calculations: her son might be twelve, if she'd been so young at his birth. He was almost dizzy with relief.

'What made you go into television?' he asked, when he'd inwardly calmed down.

'Through my second husband and his brother.'

'Second—? You're married?' he demanded, descending into turmoil again.

'No, it didn't work out, and there was another divorce. I guess I'm just a rotten picker. Gerry ran off leaving a lot of debts, which I had to work to pay. The one good thing he did for me was to introduce me to his brother, Brian, who was a television producer. Brian offered me a job as his secretary, taught me everything he knew, and I loved it—the people I met, the things it was possible to do, the buzz of ideas going on all the time. Brian loaned me some money to start up for myself, and he recommended me everywhere.'

'So now you're a big-shot,' he said lightly. 'Dominating the schedules, winning all the awards—'

'Shut up,' she said, punching his arm playfully.

'You're not going to tell me you've never won an award, are you?'

His eyes warned her that he knew more than he was letting on.

'The odd little gong here and there,' she said vaguely.

'You're not the only one who knows how to use the internet, you know. You won the Golden World prize for the best documentary of the year—'

'You've really been doing your detective work, haven't you?'

'Sure—and, to show you how clever I am, I know how to use a telephone as well.'

'No kidding?'

'I made a few calls last night and spoke to someone who knows your work and admires it.'

He didn't add that his friend had known

nothing about her personal life. It had been a frustrating call.

'He mentioned a big new project you were gearing up for, but he didn't know any details. He just said glumly, "I suppose the rest of us can give up for the next year, while she walks off with everything in sight."'

'You've been checking up on me with a vengeance,' she said, laughing at him with her head on one side.

'Which makes us quits, since you came to look me over.'

'You were recommended to me so strongly and by so many people that I started to get a bit cross with you. I must admit that I half hoped to find that you were useless. But you were quite the reverse, and that made me even more annoyed.'

'So you've reluctantly decided to offer me a job? How about I make it easy for you and refuse?'

'Don't jump to conclusions before you know everything. I'm doing eight hour-long episodes, each one concentrating on a place where a notable event happened. I don't just need a frontman, but someone who's an archaeologist and a historian in his own right, who will have some authority.'

'You mean they're all going to be things like Pompeii?'

'One of them will be underwater.'

'Don't tell me—let me guess. *Titanic*.'

'No, the *Titanic* has been done to death. But she had two sister ships, and one of them, the *Britannic*, also sank. It was used as a hospital ship in the First World War, but it went down after only three months—probably because it hit a mine. The odd thing was that after *Titanic* went down *Britannic* was partly redesigned, to make her safer, yet she sank even faster. She's in the Aegean Sea, and there's still a lot to be learned about her fate.'

To her surprise he grew pale.

'And you want me to go down there and—?' he asked in a faint voice. 'Sorry, but that's not my area of expertise.'

'Of course not. I'll have professional divers—although you could make a trip down if you wanted to.'

'No, thank you,' he said at once.

'Not even out of curiosity?'

'Nope.'

'But why?'

'Because I'm chicken,' he said frankly. 'I'll climb any height you want, descend into any cave, but when it comes to diving in deep water—not a hope. It's my nightmare.'

'That's quite an admission,' she said, enchanted by this frankness.

He smiled, looking slightly red.

'It's better for me to admit it than wait for you to find out. So, that's that. You'll have to get somebody else.'

'Don't be silly. You'll do the frontman stuff from dry land.'

'Is that a promise? Because otherwise I'm out of here.' He edged a few inches away.

'Will you stop?' she asked, laughing.

'I just don't want misunderstandings,' he said, giving up the performance and coming closer again. 'I'm a dyed-in-the-wool coward, and don't you forget it.'

'Yeah, right. You're a coward.'

'We're all cowards about something,' he said, suddenly serious.

'I guess that's true.'

'So what's your fatal weakness?' he asked unexpectedly.

'Oh—' she said vaguely, 'I have a dozen.'

'But none you're prepared to share with me?'

'I have too much sense of self-preservation.'

'Is that how you see me? A danger that you need to be armed against?'

Looking at him, smiling and gentle, gilded by the sun that streamed through the windows, she knew he was the biggest danger she had ever faced. But she would not arm herself against him. Even if she'd wanted to, it would have been pointless.

But she kept a teasing note in her voice to say, 'Hell will freeze over before I flatter your vanity by answering that.'

'So the answer would flatter me?' he teased back.

'My lips are sealed.'

'They are now,' he said, and swiftly laid his mouth over hers.

It was the briefest possible kiss, over almost before it had begun, and then he'd risen to go to the counter, leaving her shaken. Lightly as his lips had touched hers, she seemed to still feel them there when he had moved away.

But when he returned, with more coffee, he made no mention of what had happened, leaving her free to get her bearings in peace.

'What about the third ship?' he asked.

'I beg your pardon?' she said stupidly.

'You said the *Titanic* had two sister ships. What happened to the other one?'

'She sailed for twenty-four years before being taken out of service. Nothing dramatic there. I'm still researching other places, although I've half decided to cover the battlefield of Waterloo. I'd got a file of ideas, but none of them are quite what I'm looking for.'

'You can't go by what you see in a file. You need to visit these places. I know of a few around here—it would mean going south, maybe as far as Sicily. We could set off at once.'

She looked at him. 'You mean—?'

'We'd be on the road for about a week, if you can spare the time.'

'But can you spare it? Your work at Pompeii—'

'My team know what I expect of them. They

can do without me for a few days, and I'll keep in touch.'

She was silent, torn by temptation. To be alone with him, cocooned from the real world, free to indulge the feelings that were taking her over: it was like looking at a vision of heaven.

'I could call my secretary and tell her I'll be a while coming home,' she said slowly.

'Drink your coffee and let's get out of here,' he said.

On the drive to the hotel Della sat in happy contentment. She was crazy to be doing this with a man she'd known only a day, yet she had no doubts. Everything in her yearned towards him.

She knew that by agreeing to go she'd answered an unspoken question. They wanted each other in every way. Their minds were happily in tune, but right now that was secondary to the physical attraction that was clamouring for release. She wouldn't have agreed to this trip if she wasn't prepared to make love with him. He knew it, and she knew that he did, and he knew that she knew. The knowledge lay between them, brilliant and enticing, colouring every word and thought.

When they reached her hotel she half expected him to come upstairs with her and take her into his arms at once. She would not have protested. But she was charmed by the delicacy with which he bade her goodbye in the foyer, after first greeting several people who hailed him by name.

'I know too many people here,' he said. 'It's like being under a spotlight, and that's—not what we want.'

'No,' she said.

'Tonight I have to visit my mother and explain that I'll be away a few days. I'll see you early tomorrow.'

He gave a nervous look at the receptionist, who was smiling at him, and departed without kissing Della.

CHAPTER FOUR

CARLO was there next morning, before she had quite finished her breakfast, spreading the map before her, and explaining that Italy was divided into regions—'As England is divided into counties'.

'I thought we'd head for the region of Calabria,' he said. 'It's here, where the shape of the land becomes a boot. Calabria is the ankle and the toe, eternally poised to kick the island of Sicily. There are some little mountain villages full of history in Calabria that I think you'd like. After that—well, we'll see.'

'Yes,' she murmured. 'We'll see.'

They left half an hour later, heading back down the coast road they'd travelled the day before. But soon the familiar scenery was behind them. The further south they went the more conscious she became that Italy had been one country for barely a hundred and thirty years. Before that it had been a collection of independent kingdoms and provinces, and even now the extreme north and south seemed to be united only in name.

Calabria was like another world—so different that it was sometimes known as the real Italy, Carlo told her. In contrast to the sophistication of the elegant northern regions, here there was wildness, even savagery in the countryside. The mountains were higher than anywhere else, their sides dotted with medieval towns.

At last they were climbing, going so high up a mountain road that she hardly dared to look, and finishing in a small, ancient village, with cobble-stones and one inn. As he brought the car to a halt Carlo gave her a questioning smile, which she returned, nodding.

'What is this place called?' she asked.

'I didn't notice. It's so tiny it may not even have a name.'

That made everything perfect—an unknown place, set apart from the rest of the world, where they would find each other.

A cheerful man in shirtsleeves appeared as they entered. In answer to Carlo's query, he confirmed that he had two vacant rooms, one large, one small.

'The small for me, the large one for the lady,' Carlo said.

A perfect gentleman, she thought, charmed by his refusal to take her for granted, even after the understanding that had passed between them.

Their doors were immediately opposite, on a tiny landing, so that she gained a brief glimpse of his bedroom with its single bed, so different from the huge double one in her own room.

They were the only guests. Donato, the proprietor, said that his wife would cook whatever they liked, so they dined on macaroni and beans in tomato soup, pickled veal, sausage with raisins, and *cuccidatta*—cookies filled with figs, nuts and raisins—washed down with the full bodied wines of the area.

They talked very little, because their table soon became the focus of attention. Every few minutes one of Donato's two pretty daughters would appear, to ask if there was anything else they wanted. Before leaving they would give the handsome Carlo a lingering look.

Della choked back her laughter while he buried his face in his hands.

'I expect this happens everywhere you go,' she said.

'What do I say to that? If I agree I sound like a conceited jerk.'

'And if you disagree it wouldn't be true.'

'Can we drop the subject?' he asked through gritted teeth.

'I've been watching the girls giving you the glad eye everywhere we go. Some of them are being hopeful, of course, but some look as if they're trying to remind you of something.'

He had the grace to blush, but said nothing for a while. When he finally spoke it was in a different voice.

'That was another life,' he said quietly. 'Too many passing ships—but that was just it. They all passed on their way, leaving no trace *here*.' He laid his hand over his heart.

Then he refilled her glass, and didn't look at her as he asked, 'What about you?'

'Two husbands, a child and a career,' she reminded him. 'I've had no time for distractions.'

'I'm glad,' he said quietly.

There was no mistaking his meaning. She met his eyes and nodded.

Soon after that they rose and went slowly upstairs. At his door he paused, half turning, waiting for her to make the next move. She put out her hand to him.

'Come,' she whispered.

He came to her slowly, as if unable to believe what was happening. She took hold of him, drawing him into her room and closing the door behind him, not putting on the light. With the curtains drawn back at the tall windows the moonlight came softly in, holding them in its glow while they stood, entranced.

His fingertips brushed her cheek softly, and it was the sweetest feeling she had ever known. She wanted him now with her whole body. Every inch of her was eager for him to hurry, to take her to the next moment of passion, and from there to the next.

Yet, contrarily, she wanted to prolong the leisurely tension of this moment, enjoying it to the full before it dissolved into urgency. He seemed to want the same, because he laid his lips over hers with a gentleness that suggested he was in no hurry. She leaned against him and felt his fingers in her hair, while his mouth explored hers slowly.

She relaxed into the kiss, letting it invade her subtly, then offering it back with all of herself. She began to explore his body, finding it just as it had been in her dreams: hard, strong, and all hers. He wanted her more than he could bear, and that knowledge was the sweetest aphrodisiac.

Neither knew who first began to undress the other, but her fingers were working on his buttons just as he was doing the same for her. Every moment there was some new revelation— smooth skin, a seductive curve—all managed in leisurely fashion until suddenly the delay became unbearable and they started to hurry. The hurry became urgency, and they had reached the bed before they'd quite finished undressing each other. There was barely time to strip off the last garments.

As passion mounted she became less aware of

his gentleness and more aware of his vigour. For her sake he'd restrained himself until the last moment, but now he was beyond even his own control, and he held her in a strong grip as he moved over her, claimed her totally.

She had lived without lovemaking long enough to find the experience unfamiliar, but even as distant memories returned she knew that nothing had ever been like this. No other man had held her with such urgency and reverence combined, or taken her as deeply, satisfyingly, powerfully. It was like being reborn, or born for the first time.

Nothing had ever been like it before, and nothing would ever be like it after him. She knew that even then.

When their moment came he looked into her eyes, seeking complicity as well as union. Two of them became one, then two again, but not the same two. Now she was a part of him, as he was a part of her, and would always be. And that had never been true before.

He slept first, like any healthy animal whose senses had been satiated. For a while Della lay still, enjoying the weight of his head against her breasts, the gentle pleasure of running her fingers through his hair, the warmth of his breath against her skin.

The whole sensation was unbearably sweet; so unbearable that after a while she slid away from under him and left the bed. She could not think straight while his warm, loving body was nestled against hers.

She went to the window and stood looking out into the darkness, not thinking, letting her feelings have their way with her. But eventually she managed to order her thoughts.

I suppose I'm crazy, but so what? I love him, and I'll always love him, but it won't last. We'll have this little time together, then go our separate ways—because that's what has to happen. He'll tire of me and find someone else, and that's fine. The only heart broken will be mine. And that's fine, too.

But when she awoke next morning all thoughts of broken hearts were far away. She opened her eyes to find Carlo propped on his elbows, looking down at her.

He was almost smiling, but there was also a

question in his eyes, and with a sense of incredulity she realised that he was apprehensive. Last night he had been a confident lover, seducing her with practised skill. This morning he was unsure of himself.

Slowly she raised a hand and let her fingers drift down his cheek

'Hallo,' she whispered, smiling.

He got the message, his face brightened, and the next moment he'd seized her into his arms, crushing her in an exuberant hug, laughing with something that sounded almost like relief.

'No regrets?' he whispered.

'No regrets.'

'You don't want to turn back?'

He might have meant on their journey, but she understood his true meaning. They'd started on another journey, to an unknown destination. She'd made her mind up before this, but after a night of joy in his arms nothing would have held her back. Wherever the road led, she was ready and eager for it.

As they left the hotel he saw her giving yearning looks at his car.

'If you were a gentleman you'd offer to let me drive,' Della sighed,

It was comical how swiftly the ardent lover vanished, replaced by a man guarding his treasure like a lion defending its young.

'An Italian car on Italian roads?' he said, aghast.

'I've driven in France,' she told him. 'So I have an international licence, and I'm used to driving on the wrong side of the road.'

He glared. 'It's the English who drive on the wrong side of the road. And this is my *new* car. Forget it. I'm not that much of a gentleman.'

'I was afraid of that,' she said sorrowfully.

'Get in—the *passenger* seat.'

She assumed a robot voice to say croakily, 'I obey!' That made him grin, but he didn't yield. Not yet.

He headed the car down the hill and drove for an hour, before pulling up in a quiet country lane and demanding to see her international licence, which he examined with all the punctilious care of a beaurocrat.

'It's a clean licence,' she pointed out. 'It says that I'm absolutely safe to drive on continental roads.'

'It says nothing of the kind,' he growled. 'It simply says you haven't been caught out yet.'

'You're not very gallant.'

'No man is gallant where his new car is concerned. This licence doesn't mean anything. The English give them out like confetti. That's how little road sense they have.'

'Or I might have forged it,' she offered helpfully.

He gave her a dark look and got out of the car.

'Five minutes,' he said. 'That's all.'

He instructed her in the vehicle's finer points and they set off. Five minutes became ten, then half an hour. She was instantly at home in the lovely vehicle, for fast, expensive cars were her secret weakness. In England she didn't even own a car, since life in central London made it impractical, so this was a treat that seldom came her way, and she made the most of it, feeling her sedate, respectable side falling away with every mile.

Even Carlo had to admit that she was a natural driver. He might groan all he pleased, but she could sense him relaxing beside her as her skill became increasingly clear.

'Well, I suppose you're not too bad,' he said at last.

'Thank you,' she said wryly.

'All right—you're much better than I expected, and I'm sorry I doubted you.' Then he ruined the effect by saying, 'But let's stop for lunch while my nerves can stand it.'

She chuckled, and pulled into an inn that had appeared just ahead.

After lunch he reclaimed the driver's seat, and as they continued south he explained about Badolato, their next destination.

'It's near the coast. I know it pretty well because I've been researching the Holy Grail.'

'Here? But surely the Grail is—?' she stopped.

'That's the point. Nobody knows where it is— or even what it was. But supposedly the Knights Templar used Badolato as a base, and they brought the Grail to the town for a while. Some people say it's still there, hidden.'

'You believe that?'

'I believe it's a very curious place. There are thirteen churches for a population of three and a half thousand, and the purity of the spring water is legendary. People come from miles around to fill up on it. They come to swim, too. It has its own beach down below, and the town is just above. In fact, there it is.'

She looked up and saw a medieval village rising steeply on the hillside in the distance.

'I called ahead to the hotel where I normally stay,' he said.

'I hope you booked only one room this time?'

He grinned. 'Yes, I did.'

Then she saw the beach.

'It's perfect!' she breathed. 'I've never seen such white sand or such blue sea—no, not blue. It's practically violet.'

'That's a common trick of the light, especially this late in the afternoon. Shall we stop?'

'Oh, yes, please. I'm dying for a swim.'

She felt sticky after the drive. Luckily the Badolato Marina was geared for bathers, and they were able to secure a hut. A run down the beach, a plunge into the surf, and all practical cares fell away as though the sea had washed them to oblivion.

She had discovered his body in the darkness,

and knew the feel of every inch, but seeing it in sunlight was a new pleasure. She felt a guilty, almost voyeuristic pleasure in watching him as he plunged in and out of the water. It was like finding valuable treasure and securing it for her private enjoyment.

'What is it?' he asked, finally noticing her standing back and regarding him.

'I'm just appreciating the view, thinking my thoughts.'

'Tell me about those thoughts.'

She laid a hand on his chest, letting her fingers walk down a few inches.

'Those kind of thoughts,' she said.

'Don't do that,' he said in a shaking voice.

She withdrew her hand and stood, giving him a challenging look, with her head on one side.

'And don't do that either,' he begged. 'This is a public place.'

She laughed, having fun. But suddenly she became aware that the light had faded and the air was rapidly growing colder. It had happened all in a moment.

'Come on,' he said.

Grabbing her hand, he dashed for the shore, while the sky darkened still, and growled until it exploded into a bang that almost deafened her. They changed in a hurry and reached the car as the first lightning flashed. She managed to get there first, and opened the driver's door.

'It's better if I drive—' he started to say.

'Get in.'

He had to move fast, and then they were swinging out of the car park and up the hill. At once Della knew the task was harder than she'd reckoned. The road seemed to wind and wind, and it took all her attention to stay steady. Then the rain came crashing down about them, making the journey even more hair-raising.

Luckily it was only a brief drive, and within a few minutes they'd reached Badolato.

'Turn left just there,' Carlo said in a grim voice. 'Then right.'

She did so, and drew up outside a modest but comfortable-looking hotel.

Carlo threw her a sulphurous look, but said nothing until she had switched off the engine. Then he exploded.

'*You stupid woman!*'

'I'm sorry,' she said.

'What on earth came over you? Do you think driving up a steep, winding road in a thunderstorm is—is—?' He became speechless.

'I honestly don't know what came over me. It's so unlike me to go mad like that. I'm usually so sensible.'

'Sensible! Hah! More like five years old. Did I say something funny?' he added sharply, because Della's lips had twisted into a smile.

'Well, I'm a lot more than five years old,' she said wryly. 'Carlo, I'm truly sorry for going crazy like that, but nothing happened. There isn't a scratch on your car.'

'Be damned to the car!' he roared. 'Do you think that's what—?'

'And I didn't hurt anyone else.'

'We're lucky we didn't meet anything coming down the hill.'

'Hey, I'm a good driver.'

'You're a blithering idiot,' he snapped, not mincing matters. 'I've seen children with more sense. You—you—'

He jerked her roughly into his arms and held her close in a grip of iron. She could hardly breathe, but she could feel, with relief, that what drove him was no longer rage but a kind of hair-tearing distraction.

'You could have been killed,' he said in a muffled voice against her neck. 'And don't give me that nonsense about being a good driver. You're not as good as that—d'you hear?'

He drew back, holding her face between his hands so that she could see his eyes, dark with something that was almost desperation.

'Don't you ever dare give me a fright like that again,' he said fiercely. *'Mio dio!'*

She was still partly in the grip of the wild mood that had seized her, and it was being driven higher by the lightning that flashed through the window, the thunder that almost seemed to be in the car with them. But most potent of all was the way he was trembling, as conflicting feelings raged within him.

'If you ever dare do that again—' he said hoarsely.

'Yes—what—?'

'Come here.'

'Tell me what'll happen if I do it again,' she whispered provocatively.

'I said come here.'

So she did. She did everything he wanted, laughing and singing within herself, so that her spirit soared and everywhere the world was full of joy.

'I'm in love with you. You know that, don't you?'

'Hush!'

'Why? Aren't I allowed to say it?'

'Carlo, be sensible—'

'Not in a million years.'

'But three days—'

'Three days, three hours, three minutes. What does it matter? It was always there, wasn't it? As soon as I saw you there at Pompeii, when I heard you laughing—'

'When I saw you clowning around for those kids—'

'Is that why you love me? Because I can make you laugh?'

'Hey, cheeky! I didn't say I loved you.'

'But you do, don't you? Let me hear you say it—please, Della.'

'Hmm!'

'Say it, please. Don't tease me.'

'Be patient. Three days is too soon.'

'Say it.'

'Too soon…'

They spent the day in Badolato, with Della making notes and buying up all the local books she could find. When evening came they ate in their room, preferring to hide from the rest of the world. But tonight only half her attention was for Carlo. What she had seen today had fired her imagination.

'It's promising,' she said, flicking through her notes. 'If I can only find a few more like this.'

'Come and have a shower,' he urged. 'It's time we were thinking of bed.'

'Yes, but don't you see—?'

'We can talk in the shower,' he said, beginning to undress her.

But in the shower there were other distractions, and by the time they had lathered and rinsed each other the conversation was no further advanced.

'This is supposed to be a working trip,' she murmured when they were lying naked in bed.

'We've spent all day working,' he complained, brushing one finger over the swell of her breast.

'But I haven't got enough for the series,' she said, trying not to let her voice shake from the tremors going through her.

'What are you looking for?' he asked. 'Do you just want tragic places, like Pompeii and the sunken liner, or dramatic, mysterious places like this?'

His own voice shook on the final words, because her hand had found him, the fingers caressing him softly in a way that made it hard for him to concentrate.

'But what else is there?' she asked.

'Cheerful places.'

'Are there any?'

'Don't you know your own country's history? What about The Field of the Cloth of Gold?'

She frowned. 'Wasn't that—?'

'If you wanted to be pompous you could call it the first great summit conference, but actually it was just a jumbo jolly.'

'A jumbo jolly?' She chuckled. 'I like that.'

'Four hundred years ago King Henry VIII of England and Francis I of France, plus their courts, met in a field outside Calais. They put up huge tents made of silk, satin and gold, and had a party that was so extravagant that the locals celebrate it to this day.'

He slid further down in the bed beside her, stroking the inside of her thigh in a way that made it hard to remember that she was supposed to be working. She tried to apply her mind.

'I thought you said it was a summit conference,' she gasped.

'Officially it was about forging an alliance,' he murmured against her warm skin, 'but actually it was jousting by day, and wine, women and song in the evening. Francis and Henry were young men in their twenties, who still knew how to have fun. It went on for three weeks.'

'Three weeks—?'

'Then they had a wrestling match, and Henry landed flat on his royal ass. After that he decided it was time to go home.'

'Very wise,' she said in a daze. 'You know what I think?'

'What?'

She reached for him. 'I think, to hell with Henry VIII.'

From there they drove further south, to the toe of Italy, from where they took the ferry to Sicily. They spent a day in Palermo, where Carlo underwent a transformation worthy of a sci-fi plot. The playboy disappeared, and in his place was the academic, enthused by being in one of his favourite places, eager to make her see it through his eyes. But for once he forgot to tailor his words to his audience.

'What are you looking at?' he asked once, seeing her staring into the sky above.

'Trying to follow a word you're saying,' she said plaintively. 'It's all up there, above my head.'

'Sorry, I'll make it simpler.'

'You'll have to when you're writing a script—but forget it for now. Can't you talk anything but that serious stuff?'

'I was auditioning,' he said, sounding hurt.

'Don't call me, I'll call you,' she chuckled. 'But I have something different to say.'

He looked mischievously into her eyes. 'What would that be?'

'Something you don't need words for.'

He took her hand. 'Let's go.'

After that they more or less abandoned the idea of work. They spent the days exploring the scenery, the evenings over softly lit dinners, and the nights in tiny hillside hotels with nothing to think of but each other. It became indistinguishable from a holiday, and that was how she told herself to think of it—a perfect time, separate from the real world, to be looked back on later with nostalgia but no regret.

She took a hundred photographs, to last her through the years, and congratulated herself on being sensible.

'It's been a few days. Have I known you long enough yet to love you?'

'You're a very impatient man.'

'I always was. When I want something I want it now. And I want you. Don't you feel the same?'

'Yes—'

'Then can't you say that you love me? Not just want, but love.'

'Be patient. It all seems so unreal.'

'Loving you is the only reality. I've never loved any woman before. I mean that. Casual infatuations don't count against what I feel now. I was waiting for you, for my Della—because you've always been mine, even before we met—*my* Della, the only woman my heart will ever love, from this time on. Tell me that you believe me.'

'I do believe you. I can feel your heart beneath my hand now.'

'It's all yours, now and for ever.'

'Hush, don't talk about for ever. It's too far away.'

'No, it's here and now, and it always will be. Tell me that you love me—'

'Not yet—not yet—'

'Say it—say it—'

CHAPTER FIVE

DELLA sometimes wondered if the dream would have gone on for ever if blunt reality hadn't dumped itself on them.

'That was my brother Ruggiero,' Carlo said reluctantly, as he finished a call on his cellphone. 'Reminding me that he and I have a birthday in a few days, and there's going to be a family party. If I'm not there, I'm a dead man.'

Reluctantly they turned back, took the ferry across the Strait of Messina, and headed north. On the way Della called the Vallini and booked a room.

It was nearly eight in the evening before Carlo dropped her at the door.

'I must look into my apartment,' he said, 'pick up any mail, call my mother, then shower and make myself presentable. On second thoughts, reverse those two. I'll call her when I'm presentable.'

'But on the phone she can't tell if you're clean and tidy or not.'

He grinned. 'You don't know my mother. I'll be back in an hour.'

He kissed her briefly and departed. As the porter carried her bags upstairs she tried to be sensible. Their perfect time together was over. Now she would do as she had always assured herself, and return to the real world.

But not just now. It could wait another night.

Standing at her window, she could just make out the sight of his car vanishing down the road. So much for common sense, she told herself wryly. But she'd be strong tomorrow. Or perhaps the day after.

As they'd travelled she had purchased some extra garments to supplement the meagre supply she'd brought from England, but now she had nothing that was not rumpled. She unpacked, trying to find something for that evening, but it was useless.

A knock on the door interrupted her musings. Wondering if Carlo could have returned, she hurried to open it.

It wasn't Carlo who stood there, but a heavily built young man, beefily handsome, with a winning smile.

'Sol!' she cried in delight, opening her arms to her beloved son.

'Hallo!' he said, enveloping her in a huge hug and swinging her around while he kicked the door shut behind him.

'What are you doing here?' she asked at last, standing back to survey him with pleasure.

'I came to see you. You've been away much longer than you said.'

'Yes, well—something came up—all sorts of new ideas that I thought I should investigate.' She had an uneasy suspicion that she was floundering, and finished hastily, 'But I explained all this to you on the phone.'

'Yes, you talked about a few extra days, but you were supposed to return to Naples yesterday. In fact, you originally said you'd be back in London last week.'

'How is your father these days?' she asked quickly.

'Making a fool of himself with a new girlfriend. I was definitely in the way, so I went home and called Sally.'

'Sally?' She frowned. 'I thought she was called Gina?'

'No, Gina was the one before.'

'I can't keep track. So Sally's the latest?'

'*Was* the latest. It was never going to last long and—' he gave a casual shrug, 'it didn't. So, since I had a few days free, I thought I'd like to spend some time with my mother, and I came to Naples to find you.' He sighed forlornly. 'Only you weren't here.'

'Don't you give me that abandoned orphan voice,' she said, trying not to laugh.

'Then don't you try to change the subject.' He stood back and eyed her mischievously. 'Come on—tell me. What have you been up to?'

'Oi, cheeky!' she said, poking him gently in the ribs and hoping she didn't sound too self-conscious. 'I've spent a few days with Signor Rinucci, to assess him for the programme.'

'You don't usually have to go to these lengths to audition someone.'

'This is different. He's not just going to be the

frontman. He's an archaeologist and a historian, with a big reputation, and he's been showing me several new sites.'

'I can't wait to meet him,' Sol declared, with a touch of irony that she tried to ignore.

'He'll be here in an hour. We can all have dinner together—'

'Ah, well—I've actually made a few plans…'

'You've got a new girl already? That's fast work, even for you.'

'I met her on the plane—she's scared of flying, so naturally I—'

'Naturally,' she agreed, chuckling.

He glanced at the open suitcase on her bed, and something seemed to strike him.

'Did you bring enough clothes for your jaunt?'

'I was just thinking that I need to buy something new in the boutique downstairs.'

'Great idea,' he said heartily. 'Let's go.'

She'd been his mother long enough to be cynical, and had the reward of seeing her darkest suspicions realised when the boutique turned out to be unisex, and he headed for an array of dazzling male Italian fashions.

Della smiled, and observed him with pride. After all, what were mothers for?

'You should try this,' he said, belatedly remembering her and indicating a black cocktail dress of heartbreaking elegance.

But the price tag made her blanch.

'I don't think—'

'Aw, c'mon. So it's a bit pricey? So what? This is Italy's greatest designer, and you'll look wonderful in it. I'll boast to everyone we meet—hey, that's my mum!'

'And it'll make your purchases look thrifty by comparison,' she teased.

'I'm shocked by your suspicions. You cut me to the heart.'

'Hmm! All right—I'll try it on.'

Rather annoyingly, the dress was perfect, and she longed to see Carlo's eyes when he saw her in it.

'Was I right, or was I right?' Sol demanded as she paraded around the shop.

'You were right, but—'

'But it kills you to admit it,' he said, giving her the grin she adored.

It was a constant surprise to her that this son of

a boring, commonplace father could be so well endowed with charm. She knew his faults. He was selfish, cocky, and thought his looks and appeal meant the world was his. If the world didn't offer, he would reach out and take, paying his debt in smiles.

But they had been companions in misfortune almost since the day of his birth. Whatever had happened, he'd been there, with his cheeky grin and his hopeful, 'C'mon, Mum, it's not so bad.'

There had been times when his resilience and his ability to make her laugh had been her chief strength. She'd clung to him—perhaps too much, she sometimes thought. But he'd always been there for her, and now nothing was too good for him.

'Oh, come here!' she said, flinging her arms wide. 'Don't ask me why I love you. I suppose there's a reason.'

Carlo got through everything there was to do in his apartment in double-quick time, sorting through the mail and ruthlessly tossing most of it aside as junk. He called his mother to let her know he was back, and promised to be at the villa punctually the following evening.

'I shall have a lady with me,' he said cautiously.

'Well, it's about time,' Hope Rinucci replied robustly.

That startled him. This wasn't the first woman he'd taken home, so he could only assume that something in his tone had alerted Hope to the fact that this guest was different. She was the one.

He hung up, thinking affectionately that the man who could bottle a mother's instinct and market it would be a millionaire in no time.

Having showered, he drove back to the Vallini, looking forward to the evening ahead. They had just spent over a week living closely together, but after little more than an hour away from her he found that the need to see her again was almost unbearable. At the hotel he parked the car and ran into the foyer, like a man seeking his only hope on earth.

The way to the elevators took him past the hotel boutique. He stopped, checked by a sight that sent a chill through him.

Della was there, wearing a stylish black cocktail dress that she was showing off to an extremely good-looking young man who looked to be in his early twenties. He was watching her with his head on one side, and they were laughing at each other. As Carlo stared, feeling as though something had turned him to stone, Della opened her arms wide. The young man did the same, and they embraced each other in a giant hug.

He heard her say, 'Don't ask me why I love you. I suppose there's a reason.'

Carlo wanted to do a thousand things at once—to run away and hide, pretend that this had never happened, and then perhaps the clock would turn back to before he'd seen her in the arms of another man. But he also wanted to race up to them and pull them apart. He wanted to punch the man to the ground, then turn on Della and accuse her, with terrible bitterness, of breaking his heart. He wanted to do all the violent things that were not in his nature.

But he did none of them. Instead, almost without realising that he was moving, he went to stand in front of them. It was the young man who saw him first.

'Hey, I think your friend's here,' he said cheerfully.

Della looked up, smiling, but making no effort to disentangle herself from the embrace.

'Hallo, darling,' she said. 'You haven't met my son, have you?'

Carlo clenched his hands. Her son! Who did she think she was kidding?

'Very funny,' he said coldly. 'How old were you when you had him? Six?'

The young man roared with laughter, making Carlo dream of murder.

'It's your own fault for looking so young,' he told her.

She chuckled and disengaged herself.

'I was sixteen when Sol was born,' she told Carlo. 'I told you that once before.'

'Yes, but—' Carlo fell silent.

'And he's twenty-one now,' she finished. 'He looks older because he's built like an ox.'

Sol grinned at this description and extended his hand. Dazed, Carlo shook it.

'We had no idea you were coming,' he said, appalled at how stupid the words sounded. But stupid was exactly how he felt.

'No, I thought I'd drop in and pay my old lady an unexpected visit,' Sol said cheerfully. 'I thought she'd only be here for a couple of days. When she didn't return I decided to come and see what mischief she was up to.' His ribald glance made it clear that he'd already formed his own opinion.

Carlo decided that he could dislike Sol very much if he put his mind to it. But he forced himself to say politely, 'I hope you'll stay long enough to visit my family? We're having dinner with them tomorrow night, and of course you must join us.'

'Love to. Fine—I'll be off now.' He kissed Della's cheek. 'I'm in the room opposite yours. See ya! Oh—yes…' He seemed to become aware that the staff were nervously eyeing his new shirt.

'It's all right,' she told them. 'You can put it on my bill.'

'Bless you,' Sol said fervently. 'Actually, I found a few other—'

'Put them *all* on my bill,' she said, amused and resigned. 'Now, be off—before I end up in the Poor House.'

'Thanks!'

Halfway to the door, he stopped. 'Um…'

'What *now?*'

'I hadn't realised what an expensive place this is—' He broke off significantly.

'You've got a new credit card,' she reminded him.

'Ye-es, but—'

'You can't have hit the limit already. Even you.'

His response was a helpless shrug, topped off by his best winning smile. Carlo watched him closely.

'Here,' Della said, reaching into her bag and producing a handful of cash. 'I'll call the card company and underwrite a new limit.'

'Thanks, Mum. Bye!'

He vanished.

'I'll be with you in a moment,' Della said, and went into the changing room.

After a moment she emerged in her street clothes, paid her bill, and gave her room number for the dress to be delivered.

'And the other things, for the young man?' the assistant asked.

'Oh, yes—deliver them to me, too.'

A brief glance at the paperwork showed Carlo that she had spent about ten times as much on Sol as on herself.

They left the boutique and headed for the coffee bar next door. Carlo seemed thoughtful, and she guessed that he now had a lot to think about.

'Does that dress really suit me?' she asked. 'Or did Sol merely say so to get me to pay for his stuff?'

'Why would he bother?' Carlo asked wryly. 'He knew you were a soft touch, whatever he said.'

'Well, of course. Don't be fooled by the fact that he looks grown-up. He's only twenty-one, and has only just left college. Who's going to pay his bills if I don't?'

'He could get a job and start paying his own way,' Carlo suggested.

'He will, but he had to visit his father first.'

'Fair enough. But does it occur to him to curb his extravagance for your sake?'

'Why should he? When he sees me book into

one of the most expensive hotels in Naples he probably reckons I can afford a few shirts.'

He shrugged. It was a fair point, but he still didn't like it.

'Does his father help?' he asked after a while.

'His father has three other children by various mothers—the first one born barely a year after we broke up.'

'So you've always worked to support Sol?'

'I'm his mother.'

'And some woman is always going to have to be,' he pointed out, with a touch of grouchiness.

'What a rotten thing to say!' she flared. 'It's not like you.'

It was true, making him annoyed with himself.

'Ignore me,' he said, trying to laugh. 'I just got a nasty shock when I first saw you together. I thought you had another guy. He looks older than he is.'

'Twenty-one—I swear it. And I'm thirty-seven,' she said lightly. *'Thirty-seven!'*

'Why do you say it like that? As though you were announcing the crack of doom?'

'We've never talked about my age before.'

'Why should we? There were always more interesting things to do.'

'But sooner or later you had to know that I was middle-aged—'

'Middle-aged? Rubbish!' he said, with a sharp, explosive annoyance that was rare with him. 'Thirty-seven is nothing.'

'I suppose it may seem so, if you're only thirty.'

Suddenly his face softened.

'You're a remarkably silly woman—do you know that?' he asked tenderly.

'I've known it ever since I met you.'

'And just what does that mean?'

'A sensible woman would have taken one look at you and fled before you turned her whole life upside down.'

'So why didn't you?' he asked curiously.

'Maybe I didn't mind having my life turned upside down? Maybe I wanted it? I might even have said to myself that it didn't matter what happened later, because what we'd had would be worth it.'

He frowned. 'But what do you think is going to happen later?'

'I don't know, but I'm not looking too far into the future. There'll be some sadness there somewhere—'

'You don't know that—'

'Yes, I do, because there's always sadness.'

'Then we'll face it together.'

'I mean after that,' she said slowly. 'When it's over.'

He stared at her. 'You're talking about leaving me, aren't you?'

'Or you leaving me.'

'*Dio mio!* You're planning our break-up.'

'I'm not planning it—just trying to be realistic. Seven years is quite a gap, and I know I should have told you before—'

'Perhaps,' he murmured. 'But I wonder exactly when would have been the right moment.'

As he spoke he raised his head, looking at her directly, invoking a hundred memories.

When *should* she have told him? When they'd lain together in the closeness that was life and death in the same moment? When they'd walked in the dusk, arms entwined, their thoughts on the night ahead? When they'd awoken together in the mornings, sleepy and content?

He didn't speak, but nor did he need to. The questions were there, unanswerable, like a knife twisting in her heart.

'We didn't have to talk about it,' he said, more gently, 'because it doesn't matter. It can't touch us.'

'But it has to touch us.'

'Why? I knew you were older—'

'Just a little. Not that much older. And, darling, you can't pretend it didn't give you a shock. There was a moment back there when you were looking from Sol to me as if you were stunned.'

He stared at her, wondering how two people who loved each other so much could misunderstand each other so deeply. What she said was true. He had been totally stunned, reeling like a man who'd received a shattering blow.

But it wasn't her age. It had been the moment when he'd seen her in Sol's arms and thought she'd betrayed him. The extent of his pain had caught him off-guard, almost winding him. Nothing else had ever hurt so much. Nothing else would ever do so again.

It had confronted him with the full truth of his love, of the absolute necessity of his being with her and only her as long as they both lived. He'd thought himself already certain, but for a moment it had been as if she'd been snatched away from him, and he'd stared into a horrifying abyss.

And she thought he was worried about a trifle like her age.

'It's true,' she urged. 'You need to think about it.'

'I'm not listening to this,' he said impatiently. 'You're talking nonsense.'

'All right.' She made a placating gesture. 'Let it go.'

His eyes flashed anger. 'Don't humour me.'

'I just don't want to waste time arguing.'

'And I don't want you brooding over it to yourself.'

'But it's not just going to vanish—not unless I suddenly lose seven years.'

'Will you stop talking like that?' he begged. 'Thirty-seven is nothing these days. It doesn't have to bother us unless we let it.'

'Are you going to wish it away?' she asked fondly.

He shook his head. 'I'll never wish you other than you are.'

'But one day—you might.'

His response to that was to pull her close and kiss her. There were faint cheers from other customers in the little café, for lovers were always popular.

As they drew apart she smiled and sighed, letting it go at that. Now time must pass while he took in the full enormity of what he'd discovered. Already she guessed that he was beginning to understand, which was why he'd moved to silence her. Then he would realise that a permanent love was impossible, but together they would enjoy their time together while they worked on the series. It all made perfect sense, and one day perhaps it would no longer hurt so much.

The spent that evening, as they had spent others recently: dining in her room before going to bed. Over the food and wine he told her more about his family, preparing her for the next evening.

'Justin and Evie won't be there, because they live in England and Evie's heavily pregnant with twins. But Primo and Olympia will be there, and so will Luke and Minnie, down from Rome for a couple of days.'

He tactfully forbore to mention that he'd had a call from Luke, his adopted brother, now living with Minnie 'in a state of fatuous bliss', according to his brother Primo. But since Primo himself had lowered his prickly defences for the sake of the divine Olympia, he was, as Ruggiero had tartly remarked, hardly in a position to talk.

'The women are in cahoots,' Luke had warned Carlo darkly. 'So don't say you haven't been warned.'

Carlo had laughed. There was something about a family conspiracy to unite him with Della that filled him with pleasure. If only they knew how little need there was for them to nudge him into matrimony.

The thought of having Sol as a stepson made him pause, but only briefly. He would just have to put up with the young man whom he'd mentally stigmatised as 'that selfish oaf'.

He found, though, that Della was stubbornly resistant to any suggestion that her darling might not be perfect.

'What's he going to do about getting a job?' he asked mildly.

'He'll get one,' she said, a little too quickly. 'But I'm not going to hound him when he's only just left college.'

'Well, having a degree will help.'

'Actually, he doesn't have a degree,' she admitted reluctantly. 'He failed his finals.'

Carlo bit back a tart remark about that not coming as any surprise, and merely said mildly, 'But he can sit them again.'

'He doesn't think it's worth it. He says it'll be more use to look around and see a bit of the world, find out what really suits him.'

Carlo had heard this argument from lazy deadbeats too often to argue with it now. He merely observed, 'I had a job even when I was in college. There was a dig just outside town and during the vacations I slaved for hours every day, grubbing away in the earth.'

'But that's different,' she objected. 'You were doing a job you loved, making a step in your career, making contacts—'

'At the time it just felt like breaking my back

so that the whole financial burden didn't fall on my parents.'

'Well, maybe that's why he won't go back to college—to save me another year's fees.'

Her face had a mulish look he hadn't seen before, and a sudden sense of danger made him pull back. Sol could lead them into discord, and he wouldn't let that happen.

There was a new intensity in his lovemaking that night, as though he were reminding her of how good it could be between them. He had always been a patient lover, giving her all the time she needed to reach her moment. Now his consideration for her was endless, and the gentleness of his kisses as he lay with her, teasing her to fulfilment, almost made her weep.

'My love…' he murmured. 'My love for ever…'

How could she refuse a man who could make her feel like this? How could she break his heart and her own?

'Look at me,' he urged.

He had said it before. He always wanted to meet her eyes when the pleasure overtook them. But tonight it was almost a command, as if he knew the dangerous path her thoughts were taking and wanted to summon her back to him.

'Look at me,' he said again.

She did so, and found her gaze held by his as the joy mounted unbearably until they were swept away together.

One of the many reasons she loved him was that when it was over he stayed with her in both body and spirit, not turning away, but resting his head against her until he slept. It was a habit that made her feel valued as nothing else had ever done.

Tonight was no different—except that first he propped himself up on one elbow, looking down on her with worshipful eyes, as though in this way he could hold her to him. In the dim light she could just see that he was smiling.

'I guess this would be a good time to talk about getting married,' he said softly.

CHAPTER SIX

MARRIED.

The word shocked her. In her wildest moments she'd never thought of marriage. A short affair, perhaps a long affair, but not for one moment had she thought of him committing to her publicly for life.

'What did you say?' she whispered.

'I want to marry you. Why do you look like that? It can't come as a surprise.'

'It does—a little.'

'When people feel about each other as we do it has to be marriage. You're the one. I've known that from the first. Are you saying that I'm not the one for you?'

'You know better than that,' she said, touching his face gently. 'You're my love, my only love—now and for ever—'

'Good. That's settled then. We'll tell everyone tomorrow.'

'No,' she said quickly. 'That's too soon.'

'But it's a party, a big family gathering. What
could be better than telling them there's going to
be an addition to the family?'

'Well, this may seem a trifle to you, but
actually I haven't said yes.'

'Then say it and stop wasting time,' he said
lightly.

It would have been so easy to speak the word
he longed to hear and her heart longed to give—
especially now. He'd chosen his moment perfectly, for what woman could turn away from a
man who had just loved her with such fire and
tenderness? Della knew that she couldn't make
herself do that—not now, anyway.

'Let's not delay,' he urged. 'We know all we
need to—'

'Darling, we know hardly anything about
each other.'

'We know we love each other. What else is
there?'

'In a perfect world, nothing. But, my dearest

love, we're not living in a fantasy,' she pleaded. 'We're grown-up people in the real world, with real lives.'

'Are you talking that nonsense about your age again? We're the same age. We were the same age from the moment me met and loved each other, and we will always be the same. Why are you smiling?'

'I love listening when you say things like that.'

'But you think they're just fancy words? Is that it?'

It was partly true, but she didn't want to admit as much just yet.

'What will it take to convince you?' Carlo asked, moving closer in a way that suggested he was preparing for battle.

'I don't know. I expect you'll think of something. You know me so well.'

'Not as well as I'm going to. Why don't we—?'

A muffled crash from the corridor outside made him tense and look up, muttering a soft curse as they heard laughter that sounded familiar.

'He did say he was in the room facing yours, didn't he?' Carlo sighed.

'Yes, but I hadn't expected him back so soon.'

A female giggle reached them.

'There's the explanation,' Carlo said. 'He didn't waste any time, did he?'

'Don't tell me you weren't the same at twenty-one.'

'Ah, well—never mind that. Hey, where are you going?' For Della was getting up and pulling on her robe.

'He might want to talk to me,' she explained.

'You mean he'll want to find out if I'm still here.' Carlo groaned, climbing reluctantly out of bed and wishing Sol to perdition.

As Carlo had expected, Sol strolled in casually, ready to make himself at home, but his eyes were alert, taking in the sight of his mother in a dressing gown, and Carlo in the day clothes he had hastily resumed.

Della felt blushingly self conscious. She and Sol had never discussed her male friends, but there had been no need. He had never before discovered her in such a compromising position.

'Just checking that you're all right,' he told Della.

'I'm fine, darling,' she assured him. 'But haven't you left your friend on her own?'

'Yes, I must go back to her now I've said good-night to you.'

Now you've found out what you wanted to know, Carlo thought.

Aloud, he said, 'She's welcome to join us at the party tomorrow night.'

'Yes, that would be nice,' Sol said easily, rather as though he were conferring a favour.

'Did you have a good evening?' Della asked.

'Fine, thanks. Although she's an expensive little filly. So many shops stay open late in this town, and she seems to think that I'm made of money.'

'I wonder how she got that idea?' Carlo observed, to nobody in particular.

'But you managed?' Della said quickly.

'Yes—except that we came back in a cab, and I don't have quite enough to pay the fare...'

'All right,' she said, taking some money from her bag. 'Go and give him this.'

From the corridor outside came a girl's voice, calling, *'Solly—'*

'Coming, sweetheart,' he called back. Then something seemed to strike him, and he tried to return the money to Della. 'Mum, I can't leave her alone. Would you mind—?'

'Yes, she would,' Carlo said crossly. 'Your mother's not going to get dressed just to save you a journey downstairs. Do it yourself.'

'Hey, who are you to—?'

'Don't waste my time arguing,' Carlo said, seizing his shoulders and turning Sol to face the door. 'Go down there and pay the fare. Or else—'

'Carlo—' Della was plucking at his arm. 'There's no need—'

'I think there's every need. Go downstairs, Sol. *Now!*'

'Look here—'

'Clear off!'

Thrusting him out into the corridor, Carlo locked the door behind him and stood with his back to it, daring Della to object.

'You're not going to defend his behaviour, are you?' he asked.

'No, but—'

'Expecting you to go down there to run his errands? I don't think so. What's so funny?'

Della controlled her laughter long enough to say, 'But I was only going to call Reception, ask them to pay and put it on my bill. I had no intention of going downstairs.'

Carlo's face showed his chagrin.

'I suppose I made a clown of myself?' he groaned.

'No, of course not. I think it's wonderful of you to defend me. Sometimes Sol does go a bit too far.'

'Only sometimes?'

'All right, I've spoilt him. But for a long time it was just the two of us. Still, I guess I've got to learn to let go. He'll make a success of his life and he won't need me any more.'

Carlo could have told her that she was worrying about nothing, since Sol had no intension of releasing her from his demands. But he didn't want to discuss it now. It was better to take her into his arms and forget the world.

Toni Rinucci was waiting for his wife in the doorway of their room.

'I hope you're ready to come to bed now,' he said, as she reached the top of the stairs. 'You've been working all day, and tomorrow you'll be working again, if I know you.'

'Of course. Our sons have a birthday, and naturally I wish to celebrate. This will be a special birthday.'

'You say that every year.'

'But this year is different.'

'You say that every year, too,' he said fondly, beginning to undo her dress at the back.

'Bringing someone like Della Hadley to a family party changes everything.'

'Someone like? You've met her?'

'No, but I have learned how to use the internet. She's a television producer with a big reputation.'

'But surely Carlo told us that? He said she was planning a series and wanted him to be part of it, so he was taking her around to find inspiration.'

'He didn't need to be with her night and day, for over a week. Does that sound like an audition?' Hope demanded with a touch of irony. 'You think he's been sleeping with her to get the job?'

'Perhaps he hasn't been sleeping with her?' Toni suggested mildly, but backed down under his wife's withering look.

'This is Carlo we're talking about,' she reminded him.

'True—I forgot. But surely she can't be very young? Did you find out her age on the net?'

'Not exactly, but it mentioned she began to make her name a full ten years ago, so she must be mid to late thirties. Toni, I just *know* what this woman is like. To have made such a success in a man's world she must be a domineering, pushy careerist, who has contrived to beguile Carlo out of his senses.'

'But all our daughters-in-law are career women,' he protested. 'Evie still does her translating, Olympia practically runs one of Primo's factories here in Naples, and Minnie is a lawyer. Luke even moved to Rome to be near her rather than asking her to come here.'

'Yes, but—' Hope struggled to put into words her instinctive misgivings about this strange woman. 'I don't know—it's just that something tells me that she will bring bad times into this house.'

'Now you are being foolish,' he said fondly.

'I wish I could believe that you are right.'

'Come to bed.'

* * *

Myra, Sol's girlfriend, whom Della met next morning, proved to be much as expected: pretty, empty-headed, slightly grasping, but mainly good-natured. She was a native Neapolitan, and greeted the announcement that she was to go to the Villa Rinucci with a wide-eyed delight that said everything about the reputation of the Rinucci family.

As Carlo's car only seated two, a vehicle was sent down from the villa to collect Sol and Myra, which was a relief even to Della. It gave her a chance to talk to Carlo on the drive.

She was wearing the black cocktail dress, and knew she looked her best. Carlo was smarter than she had ever seen him, in a dinner jacket and black bow tie, his shaggy locks actually reduced to some sort of order. He explained this aberration by saying that otherwise his mother would make him sorry he'd been born.

'Don't tell me you're scared of her?' Della laughed.

'Terrified,' he said cheerfully. 'We all are. We were raised to be under a woman's thumb, never to answer her back, always to let her have the last word—that sort of thing. I come "ready-made hen-pecked". You'll find that very useful.'

Since this was a clear reference to a future marriage, she diplomatically made no direct reply.

'Tell me about your family,' she said.

'You wouldn't be changing the subject, by any chance?' he asked lightly.

'I might be. Maybe a man who's ready-made hen-pecked doesn't appeal to me.'

'You'd prefer to do your own hen-pecking?'

'Any woman would. That way she can ensure that the product is customised to her personal requirements.'

'True. I hadn't thought of that. I suppose reducing him to a state of total subjection is half the fun.'

'Absolutely.'

'In that case, my darling, you may find me a bit of a disappointment. I've been your devoted slave from the start, and I don't think I could manage anything else.'

'But suppose one night you come home disgracefully late and I'm waiting with a rolling pin? Surely you're going to defend yourself?'

'The situation would never arise. If I was out late you'd be with me, and we'd be disgraceful together.'

'You mean you're not going to fight me?' she demanded in mock horror.

'I don't think I'd know how,' he replied meekly. 'I was raised not to stand up to the boss lady.'

'So you won't be my lord and master?'

'Mio dio, no!'

'Come, come! Be a man.'

'If that's what "being a man" means, I'll settle for being a mouse—as long as I'm your mouse.'

There was simply no way of answering this lunatic, she thought, her lips twitching. He could make her laugh whenever he pleased, reducing her defences to nothing.

But then he added quietly, 'I've never had much use for the kind of man who feels he has to bully a woman before he can feel manly.'

His answer brought her right back into the danger area from which she'd tried to escape with humour, reminding her that it was his combination of quiet strength and gentleness that she found truly irresistible. The blazing sexual attraction that united them was only a cover. If it should die, the love would live on.

Glancing at his profile as he drove, she saw things she had missed before. The angle emphasised the firmness of his jaw, so intriguingly at odds with the meek character he'd teasingly assumed. It was at odds, too, with his easygoing nature, which she now realised was deceptive. They had never quarrelled beyond small spats that lasted five minutes, and she had almost come to think that he could never quarrel, never be really angry. The contours of his face told a different story, of a man with the self-control and generosity to keep his temper in check. But the temper was there.

The car slowed to let somebody cross ahead of them, and he took advantage of the moment to glance at her. What he saw brought a smile to his face, and she realised with a qualm that it was the smile of a supremely happy lover, full of confidence, with no doubts of his coming victory.

If she could have stopped the car and disillusioned him before his blissful dream grew stronger, she would have done so. But that was impossible, so she merely said, 'Tell me about the people I'm going to meet tonight.'

She was an only child, as both her parents had been. So she had no experience of a large family, and was curious about Carlo's. He'd previously told her about them, making them sound like a big, booming clan who were fun to be with. Now he observed that they would have dominated every part of his life if he'd allowed it.

'That's why I have my own apartment,' he said. 'So has Ruggiero, and so did Primo and Luke before they married. I adore the lot of them, but I need a place where I can behave as badly as I like.'

He spoke of the whole family, but one look at Carlo's mother told Della whose scrutiny he was really avoiding.

As they turned into the courtyard people streamed out of the villa to stand on the terrace, watching the car. Studying them quickly, Della saw a man and woman in their sixties, five younger men and two young women. They were all smiling broadly, and the smiles changed to roars of approval as Carlo waved at them.

'So you came back,' yelled one of the men. 'We thought you'd vanished for ever.'

'You mean we *hoped* he'd vanished for ever.'

More laughter, back-slapping. The man who'd said this bore a definite resemblance to Carlo, and Della guessed that this was his twin, Ruggiero.

Hope and Toni Rinucci came forward, and Della knew that she was under scrutiny. Hope saw everything. Although she did nothing so rude as to stare. Her welcome to Della was courtesy itself, her smile perfect, exactly judged.

And yet there was something missing, some final touch of warmth. Della returned her greeting, said what was proper, but her heart was not engaged any more than Hope's.

She wasn't sure if Carlo had noticed this, for everyone's attention was distracted by the arrival of Sol and Myra, who'd been travelling just behind them.

Della introduced her son, and caught Hope's startled expression at the sight of this grown up young man. After one quick glance at Della her smile became determinedly empty, as though she would die before letting the world know her real feelings.

Myra caused a sensation, being eye-catchingly attired in a dress that was low at the front, lower at the back, and high in the hem. It practically wasn't there at all, Della thought, amused, and what little there was shrieked 'good-time girl'.

More relatives appeared—Toni's brothers and sisters, aunts, cousins—until the whole world seemed to be filled with Rinuccis. Carlo gave her a glance in which helplessness and amusement were mixed, before seizing her hand and plunging in.

Della knew she was under inspection. Everyone behaved perfectly, but there was always that little flicker of interest at the moment of introduction. She became adept at following the unspoken thoughts.

So this is the woman Carlo's making a big deal about.

Not bad looking in that dress—but surely too old for him?

Once she found Hope's eyes on her, full of

anxiety. The older woman lowered her eyelids at once, but the truth could not be concealed.

A few minutes later she sought Della out, placed a glass of champagne in her hand, and said, laughing, 'I've wanted to meet you ever since I learned all about you on the Internet. When Carlo told me he knew a celebrity I was so excited.'

So Hope had been checking up on her, Della thought wryly.

'I must congratulate you on your extraordinary career,' Hope continued. 'It must be so hard to succeed in what is still, after all, a man's world.'

'It is sometimes a struggle, but there are plenty of enjoyable moments,' Della said in an even voice.

'I'm sure it must be very nice to be the one giving orders and having them obeyed,' Hope said. 'It's a pleasure that women seldom experience.'

I'll bet it's a pleasure you've often experienced, Della thought. She was beginning to get Hope's measure. It took one bossy woman to know another.

Dancing had started. Myra twirled by with

Ruggiero, which seemed not to trouble Sol at all. He was smooching with another female.

'They all act like that at twenty-one,' Della said defensively.

'Twenty-one? I'd have thought him older.'

'Everyone would,' Carlo said, just behind them. 'It's because he's built like a tank. I was exactly the same, Mamma, and you used to say I'd come to a bad end.'

As he spoke his eyes rested on Della, as if proclaiming to the world that this was the 'end' to which he had come, and he had no complaints.

'Come and dance with me,' he said, drawing her to her feet.

'It will soon be the moment,' Hope said, patting his arm. 'Don't forget.'

'The moment for what?' Della asked, as they danced slowly away.

'The exact moment we were born. Of course she doesn't know the exact moment for Luke and Primo, plus Ruggiero and I have an hour between us, so she goes for the midway point. In ten minutes' time she'll announce that it's exactly thirty-one years since we arrived in the world.'

He gave a sheepish grin.

'It embarrasses the hell out of us, but it makes her happy.'

Sure enough, ten minutes later Hope called for silence, and, standing before a huge birthday cake, made her speech. The twins exchanged glances, each ready to sink, but they said and did everything she wanted, and the rest of the crowd cheered.

'Now I'm thirty-one, and you're only six years older than me,' Carlo told Della when they were together again.

Smiling, she shook her head.

'But I have a birthday next month, and then it'll be seven again. Thirty-eight is only two years from forty, and—'

He silenced her with a finger over her lips. This time his eyes were dark, and he wasn't joking.

'I'm serious about this,' he said. 'You know we have to be together. Nothing else is possible for us.'

'When you talk like that you almost convince me.' She sighed longingly.

'Good, then let's tell everyone now.'

'No!' She clung to him firmly. 'I said *almost*. It's not as easy as you think.'

'It is,' he insisted. 'It's as easy as you want it to be.'

He was holding her close in a waltz. Now he drew her closer still, and laid his mouth over hers. It was the gentlest possible kiss and it surprised her so that she instinctively leaned into it while her body moved to the music.

'I love you,' he whispered.

'I love you,' she murmured back.

'Let me tell them now.'

Before she could answer they were engulfed by a wave of applause. As the music stopped, and he half released her, Della looked around and saw that the guests had made a circle all around them, smiling and clapping heartily.

'I think you've already told them,' she said reproachfully.

'Not in words. It's what they see that matters. Don't be angry with me.'

'I'm not, but—stop smiling at me like that. It isn't fair. You're not to say anything to anyone, you hear?'

'Is that an order?'

'Yes, it is. You said you were going to be my hen-pecked mouse, remember? So be one.'

'Ah, but that's only after the wedding,' he parried quickly. 'Until then I'm allowed an opinion of my own.'

'No, you are not,' she said firmly. 'The Boss Lady says so.'

His lips twitched, and his eyes were full of fun, looking deep into hers in the way he knew melted her.

How unscrupulous could a man be?

'So you be good,' she said, in a voice that was shaking with laughter and passion. 'Or I'll get my rolling pin out.'

For answer, he seized her hands in his, raising them to his lips, kissing the backs, the palms, the fingers.

And everyone saw him do it.

CHAPTER SEVEN

SOL appeared in Della's room the next morning, looking much the worse for wear.

'Your mother's in the shower,' Carlo said, letting him in. 'How did the rest of your evening go?'

'Nuts to it. Myra just vanished. I didn't even see her to say goodbye.'

Carlo kept a straight face. It was clear now that Myra had gone to the party hoping to snare a Rinucci, and had presumably struck gold. He made a mental note to call his brothers and ask a few carefully worded questions.

'But the car brought you back here safely?' he said, apparently sympathetic.

'When I realised that you two had already left without me—'

'We were being tactful,' Carlo assured him. 'After all, things might have worked out with

Myra—or someone else—and then you wouldn't have wanted us around. Coffee?'

Sol slid thankfully into a chair while Carlo filled a cup, then called Room Service and ordered another breakfast.

'So, what's the programme for today?' Sol said, yawning. 'I seem to be at a loose end now.'

'My programme is to spend the day with your mother,' Carlo said, speaking in an easy manner that didn't quite hide his determination. 'Just the two of us.'

Sol seemed to consider for a moment.

'That was quite a show you and Mum put up last night,' he mused.

'Be very careful what you say,' Carlo told him quietly.

'Yes, but look—just how seriously can you—? Aw, c'mon, people think we're almost the same age. How am I going to tell the world, "This is my dad"?'

'You leave me to worry about that. If you give your mother any trouble, you'll have me to deal with.'

'What do you mean, trouble? I have a terrific relationship with her.'

'Yes, you take, and she gives—and gives, and gives. I don't entirely blame you for that. I was the same at your age, selfish and greedy, but I was luckier than you. I had a twin who was as jealous of me as I was of him, plus several older brothers ready to thump the nonsense out of both of us. There was also my father, to look out for my mother. Della's had nobody—until now.'

But Sol was holding an ace, and he played it.

'If *you* give *me* any trouble, you'll have Mum to deal with,' he said.

He spoke with a touch of defiance, but it was only a small touch because he'd seen something in Carlo's eyes that most people never saw, and it made him careful.

'You could be right,' Carlo said thoughtfully.

'So we understand each other?'

Carlo gave him a brilliant grin that would have chilled the blood of anyone more perceptive than Sol.

'I understand you perfectly,' he said. 'And in time you'll understand me.'

A knock at the door announced the arrival of the extra breakfast, and by the time Della emerged from the shower Sol was concentrating on food.

'Don't question him,' Carlo said genially. 'He had a bad night.'

Della hugged her son. 'Poor darling. What are you going to do now?'

'We're going to spend the day together,' Carlo said. 'You and I need to go back to Pompeii, to start making a plan of action, and Sol's dying to come with us and hear all about it.'

The beaming smile Della turned on him effectively shut off Sol's protests.

'Sol, that's wonderful. You're really interested?'

'Of course,' he said bravely. 'I can't wait to see—everything.'

'I'll meet you both downstairs in an hour,' Carlo said, departing.

He used the hour hiring a car large enough to take the three of them. When they emerged from the elevator he hurried forward.

'I've had a call from someone who wants to discuss progress on the dig,' he told Della. 'He's waiting for me at Pompeii now, but he can't stay long so we have to get moving.'

'Oh, but—Sol wanted to do a little shopping first—'

'No time. Sorry. Let's go.'

Before anyone could argue they were in the car and on their way. Della was a little surprised, but she supposed he needed to see how the work had progressed in his absence. And she appreciated the way he made Sol sit beside himself, and talked to him throughout the journey about the fascinating tasks that awaited them.

Not that Sol seemed to appreciate this as he should. She couldn't see his face, but she could read his back view without trouble, and her lips twitched.

'You're wicked,' she murmured to Carlo, when they had parked the car and were walking to the site.

'Just wait,' he said, grinning. 'The best is yet to come.'

His team greeted him with riotous cheer, then welcomed Sol warmly. He brightened up when

Lea, a young woman in brief shorts and top, smiled at him and said, 'Have you come to help us? There's so much digging to be done. Just look at me.'

He did so. Perspiration had caused Lea's long, elegant legs to shine and her top to cling to her.

'I guess I wouldn't mind helping out,' he said, and found a trowel in his hand before the words were finished.

Carlo put his arm around Della's shoulder.

'You and I should go and consider the rest. We need to have serious business discussions.'

As he drew her away Della couldn't resist one glance over her shoulder.

'No,' Carlo said firmly, tightening his arm. 'He's all right.'

'He'll get fed up in ten minutes.'

'You do Lea an injustice. An hour at least. Forget him. From now on you belong to me.'

There was only one proper answer to this chauvinistic statement: to point out that as a modern, liberated woman she belonged to no man, and he must respect that. It must have been a moment of weakness that made her rub her cheek against the back of his hand on her shoulder, and say, 'That sounds lovely.'

They had no chance to spend the morning alone. First Carlo had to talk with the colleague who had asked him to be there early. Then he had to take the reins back into his own hands, and she listened with interest as he gave his instructions, contriving not to make them seem like orders, and generally had everything his own way by the exercise of charm.

It was an impressive performance, and it inspired her to map out this segment of the series.

They had lunch with Sol, who was hot and bothered, and not in the best of tempers.

'A strong lad like you,' she teased him.

'It's not that,' he said. 'It's just that it's boring.'

'Surely not?' Carlo said. 'My friends are very pleased with you. In fact, if you want a job they'd be glad to—'

'I don't think that's quite me,' Sol said hastily. 'I don't see myself as an archaeologist.'

'No, it takes brains,' Della teased.

'I've got brains,' he said, offended.

'Not according to your exam results,' she reminded him.

'I've told you, there was a mistake.'

'Then go back to college and take your exams again,' Carlo urged.

Sol made a face.

Renato, one of Carlo's colleagues, happened to pass at that moment, and greeted Della cheerfully. Leaning over to talk to him, she turned her back on the other two, giving Carlo the chance to say quietly to Sol, 'Then think of something else. But think of it quickly before you feel my boot in your rear. Your life is not going to be one long holiday at your mother's expense. Is that clear?'

Sol glared, but said no more. Seeing that he was thinking the situation through, Carlo left him to it.

Renato sat down to chat, and the conversation became general. Then he touched on some mysterious point relating to the dig, and within seconds he and Carlo had their heads together.

Sol took the chance to say to his mother, 'I suppose I could always go back to college.'

'I wish you would,' she said eagerly.

'What about the cost?'

'Hang the cost, if it helps your future.'

'Then perhaps I'll go home and get it orga-
nised. I think I've gone off Naples.'

Della adored her son, but the thought of a little
more time alone with Carlo was more than she
could resist.

'That's a good idea, darling.'

'What's a good idea?' Carlo asked, seeming to
become aware of them again.

'Sol's going back to college for another year.'

'That's great.'

Sol flashed a brief glance at Carlo. Della saw
it, also the bland expression that Carlo returned,
and some part of the truth came to her.

'Did I imagine that?' she demanded of him as
they returned to the dig, walking a few feet
behind the other two.

'Imagine what?'

'You know what,' she said suspiciously. 'Don't
you give me that innocent expression when I
know you're as tricky as a sackful of monkeys.'

'Well, you know me better than anyone else.'

'You fixed it, didn't you?' she accused. 'You've

been pulling strings all day. First of all you bored him to death—'

'Then I made him do some hard work. Are you mad at me?'

She opened her mouth to tell him that he had no right to interfere between her and Sol, but then a new thought occurred to her.

'No,' she conceded thoughtfully. 'I ought to be, but I've been trying to get him to return to college ever since his results came through.'

'You've been trying? But I thought you'd bought his line about looking around?'

'I pretend to believe a lot of the nonsense Sol talks because I have no choice. What did you do that I can't?'

'Scared him with the alternative,' Carlo said, grinning. 'He's a grown man. It's time he did something decisive instead of always running to Mamma. He'll be better for it, I promise you.'

'I know.'

'Come on, let's get back to town and make the arrangements before he changes his mind.'

That evening they treated Sol to the best dinner in Naples, and drove him to the airport early next day. On the drive back, Carlo said casually, 'Now we'll clear your things out of the hotel and take them home.'

'Home?'

'*Our* home.'

'I haven't said I'm moving in with you.'

'*I'm* saying it, so quit arguing.'

'And this man calls himself a hen-pecked mouse,' she observed, to no one in particular.

'I promise when we lock that door behind us I'll be as docile as you like.'

'Once you've got your own way, huh?'

'That's about the size of it,' he said outrageously.

His home was a compact bachelor apartment, three storeys up in a condominium. On two sides were large windows, looking out onto the sea and the volcano. While she was rejoicing in the view Carlo took gentle hold of her from behind.

'It seems ages since I made love to you,' he murmured.

'Shouldn't we be getting to work?'

'Everything in good time…'

* * *

After their lovemaking she assuaged her conscience about neglecting business by spending an hour sending e-mails and making calls. Then she mapped out some more plans for the series, and when Carlo awoke they worked together for an hour.

It was fascinating to see him don a new personality—serious, dedicated, knowledgeable. She'd briefly glimpsed this 'professor' before, but the change was so startling that it was almost like meeting a different man each time.

But then he would catch her eye, and she'd realise that the other Carlo hadn't gone away. He was merely biding his time. As was she.

In the afternoon they drove out to Pompeii and strolled through together, discussing camera angles and working out a script. Inevitably they ended in the museum where, after looking around for a while, Della returned to her favourite figures, the lovers curled up in each other's arms. Carlo stood close by, watching her intently, as though he could read something in her manner.

'It's such total love,' she murmured. 'Completely yielding, reducing everything else to nothing.'

He nodded.

'You wonder how they could really ignore the lava closing in on them,' he said. 'But of course they could—as long as they had each other.'

'"*How do I love thee?*"' Della murmured. '"*Let me count the ways.*"'

'What was that?' He looked at her intently.

'It's a poem, one of my favourites, written by a woman. She lists all the different ways that she loves her husband, and finishes, "*If God choose, I shall but love thee better after death.*" Elizabeth Barrett Browning lived nearly two thousand years after this couple, but she knew the same thing that they knew.'

'What all lovers know,' Carlo said. 'When you meet the woman you want to marry—that you know you *must* marry—then it's to death and beyond. If it's not like that, it isn't real.'

He was watching her in a way that suddenly made her heart pound, waiting for an answer she couldn't give.

'But this *is* real,' he persisted. 'I've known that from the start. Tell me that you've known, too. Tell me that you love me.'

It was a plea, not an order.

'You know that I love you,' she said.

He took her hand, turning it over to kiss the palm.

'How do you love me?' he asked with a touch of humour. 'Can you count the ways?'

'I'd better not,' she said tenderly. 'You're quite conceited enough already.'

But he shook his head.

'Not where you're concerned. You do as you like with me, but that's all right, as long as you love me.'

'I could never begin to tell you how much I love you.'

He contrived to put both arms around her, leaning his head down so that his forehead rested against hers.

'I think you might try,' he murmured. 'It's the only thing I want from you—no, not the only thing. There is something else—but you know that. We can talk about it later.'

'Yes, later,' she said.

He was drawing her closer to the decision she dreaded facing.

'Any time will do,' he replied softly. 'Because I know you won't refuse me the thing I want most on earth. It's what you want, too, isn't it? You've made me wait for your answer, but—'

'Darling—'

'I know, I know. I said I wouldn't hurry you, and that's what I'm doing. I'll try not to.'

'But you can't help it,' she said, trying to tease him out of the dangerous mood. 'You're much too used to having your own way.'

'That's true,' he said, his eyes glinting. 'I like to have what I want, and what I want is—'

'Hush!' She laid her fingertips over his mouth. 'Not here. Not now.'

'As my lady pleases.'

The entrance of a party of schoolchildren made them pull apart and hurry away.

For the rest of the day he was relaxed and happy, content simply to be with her. Sometimes she would look up to find him smiling, at peace with the world.

And yet it was that which made her uneasy. Clearly he had no worries—like a man completely sure of her answer. The doubts that tormented her seemed not to trouble him. She wished that she could dismiss those doubts so easily.

Soon she must have a sensible talk with him, beginning, *I'm far too old for you*—

But that wouldn't be the end, she reassured herself. Marriage was impossible, but they could stay together while they made the series— perhaps for a year. By then he would realise that she was too old for him, and things would come to a natural conclusion.

It was bliss to live with Carlo, to wake up with him, to be with him every moment and go to sleep in his arms, without having to wait for his arrival, bid him goodbye or worry about anyone else.

The only awkward note came one night when they dined at the villa. Luke and Primo had returned home, but Francesco was still there, also Ruggiero, who had brought Myra.

'It was Mamma's idea,' he murmured to Della.

'So I would have supposed,' she murmured back, amused by Hope's none-too-subtle way of reminding her that the trail led back from Myra to her grown son.

Not a word was said. Hope was too clever to

press the point, and her manner to Della could not be faulted. She treated her as a guest of honour, and let it be known in a thousand little ways that if this was her darling son's choice she was prepared to accept her.

Everyone except Myra was relieved when the evening was over. Della returned Hope's implacable smile with one that she hoped was equally resolute, and sagged as soon as she got into the car.

'Even I find them a bit overwhelming,' Carlo said sympathetically.

They didn't discuss the matter again until they were ready for bed, when she breathed out, saying, 'Your mother doesn't like me, and she's never going to.'

'It's just a passing phase because she knows you're the one and only. Nobody else has mattered like you. Wait until Sol finds his one and only.' Carlo chuckled at the thought. 'You'll be exactly the same.'

'Thank goodness he's too young for that. The college has agreed to take him back, so I'm washing my hands of him.'

'I'm glad to hear it. Or I would be if I believed it.'

Later she was to remember those remarks with irony. For now she was glad to let everything float away as she snuggled down in bed with him.

They made love sleepily, enjoying taking their time. The languorous pleasure seemed to hold her captive, making everything part of the same dream, a dream in which the world was simple.

'Say yes,' Carlo whispered. 'Say you'll marry me—it's so easy.'

He was right. It was so easy. The word hovered on the tip of her tongue. In another moment it would be said and the decision made. So easy—

Her phone rang, breaking the spell.

'If that's Sol I'll wring his neck,' Carlo growled.

And it was Sol, sounding desperate.

'Mum, is that you?'

'Yes, it's me. Sol, whatever is the matter?'

'Gina just came to see me.'

'Gina? Oh, yes—she was the one before Sally, wasn't she? How is she?'

'Mum, she's pregnant.'

Della sat up in bed. 'She's what?'

'She's pregnant. She's going to have a baby. She says it's mine.'

'Do you think it is?'

'Well—yes, probably. We were very intense for a while, and I don't think she'd have had much chance to—you know—'

'I get the picture.'

'Mum, what can I do? She says she wants to have it.'

'Good for her.'

'It's not. It's a disaster.' His voice rose to a wail. 'I'm gonna be a daddy.'

'Sol, for heaven's sake calm down.'

'How can I calm down? It's terrible.'

'We'll manage something.'

'Will you come and talk some sense into her?'

'Not the way you mean. I'll come and offer her my help and support.'

'Oh, yeah? So that she can make you a granny? Is that what you want?'

'What does it matter what I—? What did you say?'

'I said she's going to make you a grandmother. Are you going to support her in that? Mum? Mum, are you still there?'

'Yes,' she said slowly. 'I'm here. Sol, I'll call you back.'

'When are you coming home?'

'Soon. Goodbye, darling. I can't talk now.'

She hung up and sat there, not moving, sensing the world shift on its axis. Just a few words, yet nothing was the same. Nothing would ever be the same again.

She was going to be a grandmother.

'What is it, *cara*?' Carlo asked, startled by the sight of her face.

A grandmother.

'Della, whatever's the matter? What did Sol have to say?'

She remembered her own grandmother, a grey-haired elderly lady.

'*Cara*, you're scaring me. Tell me what's happened.'

She was going to be a grandmother.

'Della, for pity's sake—are you laughing?'

'Yes, I think I am,' she gasped. 'Oh, dear, I

must have been mad. Well, I came down to earth in time.' She was shaking with bitter laughter.

'I haven't the faintest idea what you're talking about.' He tried to speak lightly, but there was a nameless dread growing inside him.

'I'm not sure I really know myself,' she said, forcing herself to quieten down before she was overtaken by hysterics. 'I've been living in fantasy land—it's been like a kind of madness, and I didn't want it to end. But it had to. Now it has.'

She began to laugh again, a kind of gasping moan that drove him half wild.

'Stop it,' he said, seizing her shoulders and dropping down beside her. When she didn't stop he gave her a little shake. 'Stop that!' he said, in a voice that sounded suddenly afraid.

'It's all right,' she said, ceasing abruptly. 'My head's clear again now.'

'For the love of heaven, will you tell me what's happened? Is Sol in some sort of trouble?'

'Yes. I've got to go back to England and help him.'

'Then we must get married first. I don't want you going back until you're wearing my ring.

Don't shake your head. You were about to say yes—you know you were.'

'Yes, I was. Because I was mad. But now I'm sane again. My darling, I can't marry you. Not now or ever.'

CHAPTER EIGHT

FOR a moment Carlo didn't speak, refusing to allow her words to alarm him.

'You still haven't told me what's happened,' he pointed out. 'What did Sol tell you?'

'He's got a girl pregnant. I'm going to be a grandmother in a few months. What's so funny?'

A roar of laughter had burst from him, but he controlled it quickly, his eyes on her face.

'I'm sorry, *cara*, I can't help it. If there's one young man in the world I'd have thought would land in that kind of trouble, it's Sol. Don't tell me you're surprised. I suppose he called you to sort it out for him?'

'Carlo, did you hear what I said? I'm going to be a grandmother.'

'But why make such a tragedy of it? What are you saying? That you're going to go grey-haired and wrinkled in the next five minutes? Or are you planning to get a walking stick?'

'Don't laugh at me.'

'But it is laughable the way you make a fuss about trifles.'

'I'm going to be a granny.'

'So what? You haven't changed. You're still you—the same person you were five minutes ago. You haven't suddenly become eighty just because of this.'

'I've moved up a generation,' she said stubbornly.

'Then I'm coming with you,' he said cheerfully. 'We'll buy two walking sticks and hobble along together. Now, come back to bed. The night isn't over, and Sol's problem has given me some interesting ideas.'

He tried to draw her down between the sheets again, but she resisted.

'Will you try to be sensible?'

'What for? What did being sensible ever do for anyone?'

She loved him in this mood, but this time she couldn't yield to him. It was too serious.

'I wish you'd listen,' she said. As she spoke she

fended him off, which made him stop and stare at her, puzzled.

'I've said that you're still *you*,' he said. 'The woman I love, and will love all my days. None of this makes any difference.'

But she shook her head helplessly.

'It does.'

'But why? You haven't aged by so much as a second.'

'Haven't I? I've suddenly *seen* myself aging.'

'Because of a word? Because that's all "grandmother" is—a word.' He tried again to take her into his arms. '*Cara*, don't give in to fancies. None of this matters to us.'

He didn't understand, she realised. His words were logical, but they had no effect on the chill of fear in her heart.

'No, it's more than a word.' She sighed. 'It's a thought with a picture attached. You saw that picture yourself—grey-haired, wrinkled, walking stick. And it's made me face up to something that in my heart I've always known.'

She took his face between her hands, trying to find the courage for what had to come next.

'I fooled myself that it could work between us,' she said at last. 'What we have is lovely, and I didn't want to spoil it. I still don't. We can have everything we want—except marriage.'

He frowned, and the light died from his eyes.

'What kind of everything do you have in mind?'

'It'll take months to make the programme, and we can have that time together. Afterwards— we'll see what happens.'

There was a silence before he said, in a strange voice she'd never heard before, 'Afterwards you think I'll act like a spoilt brat who's had his fun, dumps the woman, and goes onto the next thing? That's your opinion of me? Do you even realise that you've insulted me?'

'I don't intend to insult you. I just think we should take life as it comes and not make too many demands on the future.'

He pulled away from her and got to his feet.

'No,' he said harshly. 'What you think is that I'm not sufficiently adult to make a commitment. That's what this is really about, isn't it? Behind all this "too old" talk, what you're really saying is that I'm too young—not up to standard? Why can't you be honest about it, Della?'

'Because that's not what I mean,' she cried passionately.

'Isn't it? Della, I'm thirty-one, not twenty-one. A man of thirty-one is usually reckoned mature enough to make his own decisions, and you'd see that too if you didn't have this fixation about being older. I may look like a kid to you, but nobody else would say so.'

'A man of thirty-one is still young, but I'm on the verge of middle age,' she said fiercely. 'You may not want to face it, but I have to.'

'That's a damned fool argument and you know it. Perhaps it's just a cover for something uglier?'

'What do you mean?'

'I think you decided you needed me just so long and no longer.'

Both his eyes and his voice were cold.

'Have you been stringing me along? Making a fool of me just to get material for your programme?' he demanded.

'That's nonsense. If all I wanted was research, I've got people to do it for me.'

'But not as we've done. Living it. Feeling it. And why not have a nice little vacation at the same time? He looks promising, so let's pick him up and try him out. If he succeeds as a toy-boy he may even succeed as a presenter—'

'Don't you dare say such a thing,' she flashed. 'There was nothing even remotely like that in my mind.'

'From where I'm standing, that's what it looks like.'

'I never thought of you as a toy-boy—'

'You thought of me as someone to be used—someone you could treat as a kid. I should have learned my lesson that first day, when you didn't tell me the truth about why you were in Naples. I thought I'd met the woman of my dreams, and all the time you were sizing me up, assessing whether I fitted the slot. I had my warning, but like an idiot I ignored it because—well, never mind.'

He turned and moved away from her, as though he needed to put space between them.

'You were going to keep me around for just so long, then end it when it suited you,' he said over his shoulder. 'It was nothing but a game to you.'

'I thought it was only a game to *you*,' she said wretchedly. 'It ought to have been.'

'"Ought to have been"?' he echoed, aghast. 'What the hell does that mean?'

'In the beginning—' She stopped, for emotion was making it hard for her to speak.

'Yes?' he said remorselessly.

'At the start I thought it was just a fling, for both of us. It had to be for me, and honestly I thought you were just passing the time. Carlo, be honest. Women have come and gone in your life, haven't they?'

'Yes,' he said bleakly. 'Too many. But none of them meant anything compared to you. You've always been different. I tried to make you understand that, but obviously I didn't do a very good job.'

'I thought I'd be just another of them. What we had was lovely, but I knew it couldn't last. I thought, Why shouldn't we enjoy ourselves for a while? I truly believed you'd be the one to end it. I didn't think your feelings would get that much involved.'

'You treated me as something that had no

feelings at all,' he said harshly. 'But I didn't stick to the script, did I? I fell deeply in love with you and wanted to marry you.'

Suddenly he began to laugh, but not with amusement. It had a bitter sound. 'Oh, boy! What a joke! How you must have loved that one!'

'I swear you're wrong. Carlo, listen to me. I love you more than I ever thought I could love any man, and I've tried to believe it's possible for things to work out for us. Now I know they can't.'

'I've told you I don't give a damn about your age. It doesn't matter.'

'But it'll matter later. That seven years is going to stretch. I'll be forty-five while you're still in your thirties. Then fifty. Fifty is a big milestone, and I'll pass it years before you do. You'll be in your prime and I'll be having face-lifts and injections.'

'Don't you dare,' he said at once. 'I want you as you are.'

'Darling, when I'm fifty we won't be together—'

'Stop that talk. In a hundred years we'll still be together.'

One minute they were quarrelling, the next he was laying out their future as though nothing had happened. She wanted to laugh and cry at the same time. His refusal to see the barrier between them made her love him more, but the effort of making him understand tore her apart.

'Maybe we will be together longer than I thought,' she conceded. 'I'm not saying we should separate immediately—'

'Just when the programme's complete. I'll have my uses until then.'

'No, it can be as long as you like. I won't marry you, but I'll live with you.'

'How?' he demanded. 'When the series is over we'll be working in different countries. Or are you planning to give up your career and follow me about the world?'

'I can't do that, but—'

'Or am I supposed to abandon my career and live in your shadow?'

'Of course not. But we could still find ways to be together as often as we can manage.'

'A weekend here, a weekend there,' he said bitingly. 'Until one day I turn up a day early and

you won't look up from your computer because
I don't fit into the schedule—'

'Or the day *I* arrive early and find you with
some sexy little thing who's got all the youth I
no longer have—'

'Don't say any more!'

'Why not?' she cried. 'You're bound to face the
truth one day. Why not now? It'll happen, and I
won't blame you because it'll be right and
natural. Can't you see that that's the only way we
can love each other—to be ready to let go when
the time comes?'

'And if I don't want to let go?' he demanded
fiercely.

'Then we'll stay together as long as you want.'

'You're so sure I'll be the one to break us up,
that *I'll* betray *you*,' he raged. 'You think my
love is worth so much less than yours?'

'No, I've never thought that. But those seven
years matter. I know you don't think so now, but
one day you'll see it.'

'You mean, give me enough time and I'll learn
to agree with you?' he said, with a touch of a sneer.

'When you see me getting old before you,

getting lined before you, losing my strength while you still have all yours—then—'

'Then *what*?'

She forced herself to say it.

'Then you'll realise what a mistake you've made. But there'll still be time to escape.'

'Your opinion of me is really down there in the dust, isn't it?' he asked quietly. 'All this time I thought we loved each other. But you were humouring me, treating me like a child to be indulged.'

She tried to deny it, but the words wouldn't come. Dreadful as it sounded, might this be true, even a little? She'd taken it on herself to make all the decisions in their relationship, without telling him.

On the first day she'd concealed her real purpose in being there, and then she'd concealed her age, always telling herself that she was doing it 'for the best'. Wasn't that what mothers did? Perhaps she'd had no right?

Suddenly he began to speak more gently.

'Listen to me, Della. I'm asking for more than your love. I want everything about you—the

whole of your heart and mind and your body—
for the rest of your life. I want to know that you
trust me enough to commit to me, instead of arranging things for an easy escape.'

'An escape for *you*—'

Her answer roused his anger again.

'Oh, no—that's the gloss you've put on it, but
it's your pride you're protecting. If I prove as
shabby as your expectations—well, you've
arranged it that way, haven't you?'

'I'm only leaving the door open for you—'

'No, you're practically pushing me through it,'
he raged. 'It looks generous, but it's actually a
form of control. *You* say how long we'll last, *you*
arrange the conditions of the break-up—my God,
you've even written the scene! You come back
suddenly and find me in the arms of a luscious
beauty. What then, Della? Do I stutter something
like, *You weren't meant to find out this way?*'

'Don't,' she whispered.

'Or how about, *Della, there's something I've
been meaning to tell you.* Yes, I think that would
be better. Or haven't you written my lines yet?'

He drew a long, shaky breath before continuing.

'But our love—or what I thought of as our love—isn't some damned programme you're planning, where you can cut and edit and rewrite until it's just what you want.'

She was silent, stricken to the heart by this judgement—so cruel, yet so alarmingly near the nerve.

He came close and laid his hands on her shoulders. He was in command of himself now.

'I meant what I said, Della. It has to be marriage and total commitment—or nothing. I'm not asking you to give up your career. Just relocate. You can produce your programmes from here as well as London. But I want you for my wife—not a glorified girlfriend with an escape clause, who treats me like an idiot. I want to know you trust me to be a husband, not an inferior to be guarded against because he's bound to let you down.'

'That's a terrible way to put it,' she said, aghast.

'It's how I see it.'

'Carlo, all you see is what you want. You once told me of how you go after things you've set your heart on. But you don't know the reality of marriage, and I do. I've endured two, and I know how feelings die. Not all in a moment, but inch by inch: the little irritations that loom large when they happen for the thousandth time, the moments of boredom, the times you want to bang your head against the wall, the unending day-after-dayness of it. You have no idea—'

'And neither do most people who marry,' he interrupted her. 'Follow your argument and nobody would ever get married. But they do it anyway, because they love each other enough to take the risk. And because it's how they show their trust in each other. If you don't trust me enough to marry me, then we have no future together— not even the few months you've allocated me.'

'What do you mean?' she asked, searching his face.

'I want your promise now, or it's finished. When you go to England, don't bother coming back.'

She gasped. 'You don't mean that.'

'I do mean it. You've been playing with me, and it stops here. Before you leave I want us to tell my family that we're going to be married. Mamma's expecting the announcement anyway, and we'll leave her planning the wedding.'

'My darling, I can't do that.'

He drew back, looking at her coldly.

'Of course you can't. The answer was always going to be no, wasn't it? It was no from the very first moment. It was no when everyone saw us together at the party and knew that I worshipped you. You saw what they were thinking—what *I* was thinking—and you let us all think it. You could have told me the truth at any time, and you chose not to.'

'No,' she whispered, horrified. 'It wasn't like that.'

'Wasn't it? Look me in the eye and tell me honestly. Was there ever one second when you really meant to marry me?'

'Carlo—'

'*Answer me!*'

'I don't really know what I meant. I always knew that I ought to refuse, but—'

'But it would have been inconvenient. Isn't that it?'

'No, I just couldn't bear to. It was lovely, and I wanted it to last. Sometimes I deluded myself that it might even be possible. I didn't want to admit that it couldn't happen, so I put it off and put it off.'

'Very convenient,' he said softly. 'The truth is that you made a fool of me.'

'I swear I didn't.'

'Then prove it. For the last time—will you give me the commitment I want? Because if not we have nothing more to say to each other.'

Her temper rose. 'Are you giving me an ultimatum?'

'I suppose I am.'

'Don't do that, Carlo. I won't be bullied, and certainly not into marriage.'

'I suppose that's my answer,' he said softly.

'It has to be.'

'All those nights you lay in my arms and whispered to me—all those dreams you let me indulge—you knew I was living in a fool's paradise, and you left me there because it was more convenient that way.'

'It could never last. You can't see that now because you want me—'

'Della, I am not a little kid to be protected. Don't insult me.'

'All right,' she said, tortured by this scene, unable to endure more. 'Maybe you were right when you said I'm trying to protect myself, so that I don't have to be around to see the disillusion come into your eyes. I don't want to know the moment when you ask yourself how the hell you could have done anything so stupid. I don't want to see you avert your eyes so that you don't have to look at what's happening to me. I don't want to watch you treading on eggshells because you're trying to be kind.'

There was an expression on Carlo's face that she had never seen before, and it frightened her. It was close to contempt.

'At last,' he said. 'The truth.'

'It's one truth.' She sighed in near despair. 'But there are so many different truths in this. Don't just look at that one—please, Carlo.'

His mouth twisted.

'Are you sure there's any other truth but that?' he asked, in a deadly cold voice.

After a long time she said, in a defeated voice, 'I don't know. Maybe there isn't.'

He seemed to consider this dispassionately,

before reaching for the pair of trousers that he'd tossed onto the floor last night in his haste, pulling on a shirt and walking out of the door.

For some time she sat without moving, listening for his return. She couldn't believe that he'd really left her like this. It wasn't like him.

But as the minutes passed, with no sound of his footsteps, she was forced to recognise the truth. He would not return and she had mistaken him, seeing only his sweet temper and laughing disposition, missing the steely core that had made him fight her with a touch of cruelty.

She'd been prepared for his pain, but not for his rage and scorn.

'That's the getting of wisdom,' she thought wryly. 'We neither of us knew or understood the other well. It's better as it is.'

After a while she forced herself to rise, call the airport, and book a seat on the afternoon flight to London. Then she set about packing her things, leaving out the clothes she would wear to travel while she showered.

It was finished. He would stay away until she'd left, and then she would never see him again. She said it over and over, trying to make herself believe it, accept it.

Lost in her sad thoughts, covered by cascading water, she failed to hear the bathroom door open, and had no idea that anyone was there until she turned off the water and opened the shower door. The shock caused her to slip, and she would have fallen if his arm hadn't shot out and curled around her waist, holding her firmly.

He reached up for a towel, then carried her back into the bedroom, still holding her with one arm, set her on her feet and began to dry her. He didn't speak. Nor did she expect him to. His face showed too much sadness for words.

When he'd finished she tried to take the towel, to cover herself, but he tossed it away and drew her against his chest. He hadn't bothered to do up his shirt, and the feel of his bare skin came as a shock, as though she'd never felt it before.

And in a sense that was true. In the last hour they had moved into a new world where everything was unfamiliar—everything for the first time, everything for the last time.

He drew her down on the bed and removed the

rest of his clothes so that they were naked together. She tried to protest that this wasn't a good idea, but he simply laid his face between her breasts, his eyes closed. Unable to stop herself, she clasped her hands tenderly behind his head. Whatever came later, she would have this.

He began to kiss her everywhere, murmuring softly as he did so. Bittersweet pleasure and happiness warred within her. It was the last time, but the joy of the moment was there, hot and fierce, driving out any other thought. She would love him now, and afterwards she would survive somehow.

His lovemaking was like never before, yet still the culmination of all the other times. He drew on everything he'd learned about her to increase her pleasure, calling up a storm of memories with each movement, prolonging the moments while her tension rose and she wanted to cry out for her release. But he made her wait, reminding her of how she loved this, how long the years ahead would be without the warmth of his love, asking whether she could live without it.

The answer terrified her. But she had made

her decision, and she wouldn't let him suspect that her heart was already breaking.

'Don't go,' he whispered. 'Stay with me.'

Before she could answer he entered her, moving against her with passion and tenderness until she wanted to weep. As her climax came she clung to him, looking up into his face, filled with love and fear.

Their parting was a kind of death, and brutal reality was still there, waiting, remorseless.

'Stay with me,' he whispered again. But even as he said the words he saw the desperation in her face, not what he was searching for.

'It's changed nothing, has it?' he asked bleakly.

'Nothing. I'm sorry.'

He rose and left the room without looking at her. After that there was nothing to do but get dressed and prepare to leave.

'I'll take you to the airport,' he said when she joined him.

'There's no need. I'll take a taxi.'

'I'll take you to the airport,' he repeated obstinately.

The journey was a surreal experience. They

travelled mostly in silence, and when they spoke it was about mundane matters—her ticket, her luggage.

At Naples Airport he came inside with her, watching as she checked in her luggage.

'I'm a bit late for the plane,' she said, looking anxiously at the board. 'I should go.'

'Yes, you'll have to hurry. By the way—about the series—of course I can't be in it.'

'I suppose not.'

'But you'll find another frontman,' he said coolly. 'They're ten a penny.'

Then, without warning, he broke.

'I can't stay angry with you,' he whispered. 'Della, for pity's sake, forget everything—forget what I've said—what you've said. None of it matters. Let's put all this behind us and love each other as we did before.'

She shook her head violently.

'I'll always love you,' she said. 'But it was only a dream—'

'And you can let it go just like that? Did it mean so little to you?'

'Don't,' she said, closing her eyes. 'You'll never

know what it meant to me. But we can't build a life on it, and one day you'll know I was right.'

He grasped her hand so hard that it hurt.

'But you're not right. You're taking us to disaster and you can't see it. Della, I'll beg you one last time—don't do this to us both.'

'This is the final call...'

'No,' he said fiercely, taking hold of her. 'I won't let you go. You're staying with me.'

She didn't answer in words, just shook her head in dumb misery, and at last he released her with a gesture of despair. She walked through the gate, meaning to go on without looking back. But at the last minute she had to know if he was still there, and turned slowly.

The crowd was building up, other faces passing in front of his. But she could just make him out, watching her until the very last moment, motionless, like a man whose life was ebbing away, until the crowd moved again and she could no longer see him.

CHAPTER NINE

DELLA took off from Naples in sunshine and landed in England in pouring rain. The perfect comment on her situation, she thought, if you were of a dramatic turn of mind.

Sol was at the airport, relieved that she had arrived to sort out his problems.

'Good to have you back, Mum,' he said, hugging her.

They'd had this conversation before, and her next line was, *It's lovely to be back, darling.*

But this time the words wouldn't come, and she was glad to hurry to the waiting taxi.

As they reached the houseboat Sol said, 'I've done some cleaning up, so that it's perfect for you.'

'*You've* done some cleaning up?' she queried.

'Jackie helped me a bit,' he conceded.

'Hmm!'

The place was spotless, which convinced her that this was mostly her secretary's work, but she let the subject drop. Sol was on his best behaviour—carrying her bags into the bedroom, telling her to sit down, making her coffee.

'The situation must be pretty bad to make you such a perfect gentleman,' she said, slightly amused despite her unhappiness.

'I just don't know what to think. What am I going to do with a baby?'

'I thought the idea was for me to arrange everything?'

'You're wonderful.' He kissed her cheek.

'Sure I am,' she said wryly.

With such domestic diversions she was able to fend off reality for a while. Even when she went to bed and lay thinking of Carlo she fell mercifully asleep within a few minutes. She began to think she might be let off lightly.

She discovered otherwise the following morning, when she awoke at dawn and went on deck to watch the sun come up over the river. It was a mistake. She found herself reliving the day they'd met when she'd told Carlo about this scene.

'You have to catch the moment because it vanishes so quickly.'

She'd said that, meaning the magic of dawn on the water, not knowing how perfectly the words would apply to their brief time together. The moment had come and gone, vanishing for ever, uncaught.

Now the memory would always be there, waiting for her with every dawn.

She went quickly back inside.

Nobody in the Rinucci family thought it strange that Della should need to return to England for a while. It took time for it to dawn on them that she wasn't coming back. Carlo did not encourage questions. Only to Hope did he go as far as to say, 'It could never have worked, Mamma, and we both knew it. Our careers wouldn't have fitted together.'

'Your careers?' Hope echoed, disbelieving.

'Of course,' he said lightly. 'That was always going to be a problem.'

'Can't you tell me the truth, my son?'

He sighed and gave up the pretence. 'It was the

age-gap. She made so much of it that—it was really an excuse. She didn't want me.'

'*She* rejected *you*? Rubbish!'

He managed to laugh at that.

'Unbelievable, isn't it?' he asked with a hint of teasing. 'There's actually a woman in the world who thinks I'm not up to standard.'

'Well, she must be the only one,' Hope declared, staunchly loyal. 'She's mad, and you're better off without her.'

'Yes, Mamma, if you say so.'

'Don't you take that tone with me,' she snapped.

'What tone?'

'Meek and mild. I know what it means.'

It meant that inwardly he had vanished to a place nobody could reach. Carlo, so soft-spoken and easygoing on the surface, had another self that he visited rarely and only he knew about.

Hope glared at her son, furious with him, with Della, with the world that had dared allow her darling to be hurt.

That night she confided in her husband.

'But it's what you wanted,' Toni protested. 'You never thought she was good enough for him.'

'But I meant *him* to reject *her*,' Hope said, outraged.

'He was never going to do that,' said Toni, who saw more than he said.

As if to allay their fears, Carlo began to spend more time at the villa, often staying overnight, sometimes bringing female company, but always sending the ladies away in taxis. He seemed to become his old self, laughing, flirting, always ready for a party. And the more he enjoyed himself, the more Hope's fears grew.

Once she asked him, 'Have you heard from her?'

'Not a word. What is there to say?'

'That project you were working on—?'

'Nothing will come of that now.'

'I thought—if it caused you to see each other again, then maybe…' She trailed off, not sure what she'd hoped for, but ready to accept anything that would make him happy.

'Mamma, there's no point in talking about it. It's over. Let's forget it.'

'Will *you* forget, my son?' Hope asked pointedly.

He smiled faintly and shook his head.

'No, I never will. But that's because I'm under

a special kind of curse. Forgetfulness would be a blessing, but I'll never have it, and I just have to accept that.'

Hope nodded. She, too, knew about that curse. She never spoke of it, but now she wondered if her youngest child had suspected her secret. Part of her still thought of him as the baby of the family, but now she saw that this man had a painful wisdom that he, too, kept to himself.

'*Can* you accept it?' she asked quietly.

'I can manage. And I'm damned if I'll make everyone else suffer by going around in a black cloud. We've got a lot of good news coming in this family. Justin's twins, for a start.'

'You're right,' she said. 'And yet…' She paused as she came to something that was hard to say.

'What is it?'

'I see you empty and hurting inside, and I wonder how much of it is my fault.'

'How can any of it be your fault?'

'I didn't welcome her as perhaps I might have done,' she forced herself to say. 'She wasn't what I wanted for you. Oh, I said and did all the right things. But she knew I was forcing myself, to conceal a lack of warmth inside. My son, did I drive her away and ruin your life?'

'Of course not,' he said, honestly puzzled. 'Mamma, you don't know how it was between us. Nobody could have driven her away from me—not if she didn't want to go. We had our world, and it was everything. Except that I spoiled it by—' there was a faint tremor in his voice '—by not being the man she wanted.'

'But—?'

'Try to understand this, and then never let us speak of it again. It wasn't your fault, or anyone else's except mine. In her eyes I just don't measure up. That's all there is to it.'

She understood. He was telling her, gently, that even she was irrelevant when set against his love. His eyes were kind, softening the hint of rejection, but she had no doubt that he meant it.

For a moment she hated Della with a ferocity that shocked her. All this might have been hers, and she'd tossed it away, breaking his heart, abandoning him in an endless desert.

But the man he had become understood even

this, and said quietly, 'Don't hate her, Mamma. For my sake.'

'Very well, I won't. In fact, I think you should go to England. Whatever is wrong between you put it right—if that's the only thing that will make you happy.'

It was a bad thing to say. Carlo's face was hard and set.

'Go after her?' he echoed. 'Beg from a woman who's turned me down as not up to standard? What do you think I am?'

'My dear, don't let your pride get in the way.'

He shrugged and made a wry face.

'Let a man keep his pride. It matters.'

'Well, can't I help? If I talked to her—'

She stopped before the anger that flashed in his eyes.

'Never even *think* of such a thing. Not even for a moment. Do you hear me, Mamma?'

'Yes,' she faltered. 'I won't do anything you don't want.'

For a moment she had glimpsed the fierce will inside him, and it had almost frightened her.

Carlo softened and put his arm about her.

'Forgive me for speaking to you so,' he said contritely. 'But you mustn't interfere. You can't help this situation.'

'Then what *can* help it?' she cried.

'Nothing,' he said quietly. 'Nothing at all.'

Della's first job was to visit the flower shop where Gina worked. There, she saw a pretty, tired-looking girl of about nineteen.

'Can I help you, madam?' Gina asked, but no sooner had she spoken than her eyes closed and she swayed.

Della caught her and guided her to a chair.

'The same thing used to happen to me,' she said sympathetically.

She looked up as the shop's manageress bustled out.

'I'll take her home,' she said, in a voice that brooked no argument. 'I'm her aunt.'

Gina lived in a couple of rooms a few streets away. Recognising a stronger personality, she made no protest as Della called a cab and took her away.

The rooms were much as Della had expected—

shabby and basic, but clean and cared for. Having
urged Gina to a sofa, she made a pot of tea and
sat down beside her while they both drank.

'I'm Sol's mother,' she said. 'I came to see
how you were.'

'Did he send you?' Gina asked, with an eager-
ness in her voice that touched Della's heart.

'No, I'm afraid not. I wouldn't hope for too
much from Sol, if I were you.'

'I know. He doesn't want anything to do with
the baby.'

'What about you?'

'I want it,' Gina said eagerly. 'I'm going to
have my baby, no matter what anyone says.'

Della hadn't expected to like the girl, but she
found herself drawn to her instinctively, and this
remark drew her even closer.

'Good for you,' she said.

'Do you mean that? You didn't come here to
tell me to—? I know Sol hates the idea—'

'Forget Sol. He has nothing to say about this.
He's very immature, I'm afraid.'

'Yes, he gets bored easily,' Gina admitted. 'I
know he's fed up with me.'

'Some men are like that,' Della said quietly. 'But not all of them. There are men in the world you can rely on, who want to stay with you for ever and face everything side by side.'

'Are you all right?' Gina asked suddenly.

'Yes, of course. Why do you ask?'

'Your voice trailed off suddenly, and you just stared into space.'

'Did I? I didn't realise.' She added quickly, 'Tell me about your family.'

'My mother's dead, my dad's remarried, and they don't really want to know. My mother's mother is still alive, but Dad quarrelled with her when Mum died. He said she kept interfering, and wouldn't let her visit us.'

'Then you're going to need some help, and that's why I'm here.'

She took over, arranging to pay the girl an allowance, and practically ordering her to leave work with a firmness that afterwards made her blush to recall. Luckily Gina recognised the good will behind the ruthless organisation, and was only too ready to do as she was told.

Della went home feeling happier, although slightly shocked at herself.

Bossy, she thought as she looked out at the lights on the river that night. I arrange things for people without asking how they feel.

And I never saw it until now, she added wryly to herself.

The year was moving on, and the work at Pompeii was coming to an end. Now Carlo was there at all hours, going back to his apartment to sleep, then rising early to get to work next morning. One afternoon he looked up to find Ruggiero staring at him with a baffled expression on his face.

'What is it?' Carlo asked.

'I'm trying to recognise you. What have you done to your hair?'

'Cut it off,' Carlo said, rubbing his scalp self-consciously.

'But why so short?'

'It was an accident,' Carlo said defensively. 'I spilt some goo on one side and it wouldn't wash out, so I had to cut it off, and then I had to cut off the other side, too.'

'And you did it yourself, by the look of it.'

'I was in a hurry.'

'So that's why you haven't been home for ages. You can't face Mamma.'

'Not at all. I just don't want to give her a fright. I thought I'd let it grow a bit first.'

'Get your things and come with me.'

'Where?'

'First to a barber, so that he can make you look human again. Then your apartment, so that you can shower and get presentable. Then we'll have a night out. You look like a man with an urgent need to get drunk.'

'Let's go.'

Many hours later, as the Villa Rinucci was preparing to close down for the night, Toni suddenly grew still and cocked his head towards the door. 'Can I hear singing?'

They both listened, and Hope said with wry amusement, 'I think it's *meant* to be singing, anyway.'

The next moment their twin sons appeared in the doorway, supporting each other.

'Good evening,' Ruggiero declaimed tipsily.

'Who's that with you?' Hope demanded, staring. 'Good grief!'

'It really is Carlo,' Ruggiero said. 'Although it doesn't look like him.'

'You didn't drive home like this?' Hope demanded, aghast.

'No, we took a cab,' he said, adding as an afterthought, 'Both ways.'

'So you went out knowing that you were going to get disgustingly drunk?' Toni enquired with mild interest.

'That was our intention,' Ruggiero agreed.

'Well, you might have taken me with you.'

'Next time, Poppa, I promise.'

'Stop talking nonsense,' Hope said, trying to sound stern. 'Sit down before you fall down.'

They made it at far as the sofa before Carlo collapsed and lay sprawling, his shirt open at the throat, his head thrown back, dead to the world.

Hope regarded him for a moment, trying to see the perfect picture of a happy playboy, as had happened so often before. But her mind went back to the night not so long ago when he'd slept on this very sofa after a party. That had been a man living life to the full. This was a man seeking oblivion.

Looking up, she saw the same memory in Ruggiero's eyes. A silent question passed between them, and he shook his head.

In early December the weather became much colder, and sometimes Della could barely make out the river through the rain.

She began to look forward to Christmas, when she would see Sol again and hear how his time at college was progressing.

She had become good friends with Gina, accompanying her to the clinic whenever she could, and helping her become reconciled with her grandmother. Now she had gone to spend Christmas with the old lady, and Della was alone.

She made a point of going out in the evenings. In this way she could tell herself that she was dating again, and had put Carlo behind her, but the truth was that her 'dates' were usually with men who were dealing with her professionally. Often there were four in the party.

One night in December she came home to find a light on in the boat.

'What are you doing here?' she asked, as she boarded and Sol appeared. 'Don't tell me you've been thrown out?'

'No, no—it's not as bad as that,' he said, in a soothing tone that made her heart sink. 'They just suggested that I come home for Christmas a few days early, to cool off.'

'Off from what?'

'Well, a group of us made merry. Only we had a bit too much and it turned into a fight, and— well, the police were called—'

His shrug implied that it was all a storm in a teacup, and he topped it off with a sheepish smile, designed to charm her out of making a fuss. It had worked so often before, but now she saw him through different coloured lights. He was no longer a boy but a grown man, always seeking the easy way.

'I think I'd better call the head of your college—'

'But I've told you what happened—'

'Yes, and he'll tell me what really happened. Don't take me for a fool, Sol.'

His look of surprise said clearly enough that this hadn't been a problem before. Her eyes warned him not speak.

'You'd better go to bed now, and tomorrow I'll let you know where you stand with me. Right now I'm not sure.'

This time he actually gaped.

When he'd gone to bed she sat up, brooding.

She knew that since returning to college Sol had continued to be extravagant, despite his good resolutions, but she guessed that now things were even worse. He'd accepted it as normal when she'd taken responsibility for his child. She had spoiled him all his life, damaging him in the process.

And only one person had seen it.

Carlo had known how to deal with Sol. He hadn't got heavy. He'd simply been quietly implacable, and the young man had backed down in the face of authority.

I wish he was here now, she thought. I could do with his advice.

Next day she made the call and learned the worst.

'The principal says you're a big disappointment,' she told Sol later. 'A lurid social life, and doing as little work as possible. That's it! I'm cutting off your funding. You get a job, and from now on you support yourself.'

'But I'm good for nothing,' he said, trying to charm her again.

'That's the truest thing you ever said. But even good-for-nothings can work. Get a job as a road-sweeper if you have to, *but get a job.*'

'Hey, Mum, don't give me orders. I'm not a kid.'

'As long as you're living off me, you *are* a kid. You want to be a man—earn a living.'

He gulped.

They entered into edgy negotiations. Now he had to take her seriously, as though something warned him that she'd really changed. His master stroke was to go out and get a job delivering parcels, then work himself into the ground.

He returned home triumphantly one evening, with his first wage packet.

'I haven't even opened it,' he told her virtuously.

'Good,' she said, whipping it out of his hand. 'I had a phone call today from the bank behind your credit card. Your payments are overdue. This will come in very handy.'

'But can't you—?'

'No,' she said remorselessly. 'I can't.'

Caution born of self-preservation kept him silent, and sent him back to work hard enough to make her reconsider. She relented up to a point, and when the New Year began he returned to college to 'make a new start'.

Della didn't allow herself to hope for too much, but she felt a mild sense of triumph. Sol was treating her with a cautious respect that was new, and for that she knew she had Carlo to thank.

She sent him a silent message of gratitude, wondering where he was and what he was doing. Did he ever think of her. And, if so, how?

Evie's twins had been born in late November. Carlo had entered the villa to find his mother on the phone, his father dancing a little jig of joy, and Ruggiero grinning.

He'd mouthed, 'Boy and a girl,' to Carlo.

'I'm so relieved,' Hope said, hanging up. 'The birth was a few days late and I was getting worried. And poor Justin was tearing his hair out.'

'*Justin?*' everyone cried sceptically.

Justin Dane, Hope's first son, parted from her at birth, had reappeared in their lives three years ago. In time he'd grown close to his family, but it had been hard at first, for he'd been marked by the harsh way life had treated him. He was a grim, taciturn man, who'd developed a protective shell designed to fend off human contact.

Evie's love had warmed him, so that these days he was more relaxed, and had learned how to be happy. Even so, the thought of him revealing strong emotion made the three men hoot with laughter.

'Tearing his hair out?' Ruggiero teased.

'In a manner of speaking,' Hope said. 'He says little, but I can tell.'

She and Toni departed early next morning, stayed away three days, and returned with a hundred photographs.

'Evie looks happy,' Ruggiero observed, studying the pictures.

He'd had a soft spot for Evie ever since her first visit. She was mad about motorbikes, and he'd been just about to buy a share in a bike factory, and they'd each recognised a kindred spirit in the other.

'When do we get to meet them?' Carlo asked, studying the pictures.

'They're coming for Christmas,' Hope said.

Christmas was the time the Rinuccis gathered in force. Primo and Luke returned with their wives, Francesco came over from America, Ruggiero produced a new girlfriend. And Justin and Evie came over from England with their baby twins, accompanied by Justin's fifteen-year-old-son Mark, from his first marriage.

It was he who'd brought Evie and Justin together, when she'd been a temporary language teacher at his school and he'd been her star pupil, with a propensity for playing truant. He was fascinated by languages, especially Italian, which he'd learned from her, and he loved his visits to Italy, seizing the chance to brush up not only his Italian but also on the Neapolitan dialect.

Carlo found him one day, deep in a newspaper article about Pompeii.

'Can you understand it?' Carlo asked, grinning.

'Enough to know it's about you,' Mark said.

But Carlo shook his head. 'No, it's about the site. I added a few opinions, but a good archaeologist never lets himself become the story.'

'Aren't you going to do a whole series?'

'No, that fell through,' Carlo said hastily.

'But Evie said—'

'What do you think about Pompeii?' Carlo interrupted him with a touch of desperation. 'Would you like to come and see it? I'm making my final visit tomorrow.'

Next day they drove out to Pompeii together. Mark was an ideal pupil, wide-eyed, eager, drinking everything in, responding intelligently. Carlo began in much the same way as he'd done with the schoolchildren, the day he'd met Della, and Mark enjoyed the performance. But then he said, 'But it's much more than that, isn't it?'

'Much more,' Carlo said, recognising a kindred spirit with pleasure.

He showed the boy around the whole place, talking to him as to a fellow academic, and introducing him to the team, who were finally packing up to depart. Mark was enthralled by the museum, especially the plaster figures. He lingered over the mother sheltering her children.

'How do you get on with Evie?' Carlo asked curiously.

'She's great,' Mark said at once. 'Dad's ever so much nicer now he's got her.' He giggled suddenly. 'The night we were waiting in the hospital he said he wanted us to have a talk, "man to man".'

'Heaven help us!' Carlo said with feeling.

'Yes, I thought it would be awful, but he just wanted to talk about Evie. He said when my turn came I shouldn't be in a hurry, because a man had to wait for the right person, even if he waited for years and years.'

'Justin said a thing like that?' Carlo queried, trying to imagine this from his taciturn half brother.

'Well, the twins were being born,' Mark said, as though this was a complete explanation. And Carlo thought perhaps it was.

He left Mark talking to Antonio, one of his team, and moved quietly away, brooding on the unexpected words that he'd just heard.

Even Justin had found the secret that had eluded himself.

He walked, without looking where he was going, and came inevitably to the place where the lovers still clung together—as they had done on that far-off day when he and Della had seen them for the first time; as they had still been when they were together here for the last time, when everything had seemed most perfect between them.

Nothing had changed. The lovers lay as they had done for nearly two thousand years, dead to the world but alive to each other for all eternity.

For all eternity. That was what he'd wanted, what he'd been so sure of. And he'd been wrong. He hadn't understood her for a moment.

How do I love thee…?

He could never have answered that. There were no words for how he had loved her.

Let me count the ways.

For him the ways were too many to count. For her they were too few to bother with. They had run out, leaving nothingness behind.

'I'll be going now,' said a voice nearby.

'What?' He came back to himself with a start.

'I'm on my way,' Antonio said. 'Are you all right?'

'Yes, I'm fine—fine.'
'The job's done. There's nothing to stay for.'
'No, there's nothing to stay for.'

CHAPTER TEN

IT WAS Hope who suggested to Evie that they might invite Carlo to accompany them back to England.

'He's a good influence on Mark,' she said. 'That boy's getting really interested in all sorts of serious things.'

'Yes, he's a budding intellectual,' Evie said, smiling. 'We'd love to have Carlo.'

If Carlo was suspicious of his mother's motives he kept his thoughts to himself, and agreed to the visit with every sign of pleasure. Evie afterwards said that she didn't know how she would have managed without him, as she was poorly on the flight home, and it was Carlo who took charge of the twins. This had a knock-on effect on Mark, who decided that, since his hero was happy looking after babies, it obviously wasn't unmanly after all.

On the second day of the visit Evie answered

the phone briefly, then covered the receiver to say to Carlo, 'Your fame has preceded you. Will you do a live TV show tonight? They've heard you're here, and they need an expert to talk about some new discovery.'

She named the discovery, a brilliant one by a fellow archaeologist, which had left Carlo full of envy. He accepted eagerly, and that night he arrived at the studio ready to talk. The discussion grew animated. One of the other speakers was jealous and dismissive. Carlo was up in arms, defending a man he admired. A good time was had by all.

The producer was ecstatic.

'It doesn't often get so lively,' he enthused. 'Hey, weren't you going to do that series for Della? What happened?'

'We couldn't dovetail our schedules,' Carlo said, trying to calm the frisson that went through him at the sound of her name.

'What a shame! Everything she touches now turns to gold. She's up for yet another award in a week or two. The rumour is that she'll get it.'

'I'm sure she will,' Carlo replied, not quite

knowing what he said. 'Excuse me, I have to be going.'

The visit passed pleasantly. Once Justin invited Carlo to lunch at a restaurant near his offices in London, and they talked about their mutual parent. It was the details of babyhood and childhood that seemed to fascinate him, as though he was trying to imagine a time with his mother that he'd never known. Carlo's warm heart was touched, and he did his best to fulfil Justin's hopes. By the time they reached the liqueurs they were good friends, and both inwardly groaned when there was an interruption.

'Carlo, let me introduce Alan Forest,' Justin said. 'A valued business colleague.'

Forest was a chunky middle-aged man, with a bluff, outgoing manner.

'I saw you on television the other night,' he said. 'Great stuff.'

He burbled on, impossible to interrupt. It became clear to Carlo that he had a great deal of money and, since his wife had left him the previous year, very little else. With too much time on his hands he indulged a variety of hobbies—one of which was archaeology, although his interest was amateur—and he spouted a good deal of nonsense. Carlo grinned and indulged him.

'Now, I want you and your family to be my guests tomorrow night,' Forest declared expansively. 'I've got a table for a very glamorous occasion, but unexpectedly I find myself alone.'

Since they were both too polite to say that this wasn't surprising, they merely smiled, while seeking for a reply that would get them out of the unwanted invitation.

'It's a televsion awards ceremony,' Forest burbled on. 'And it's taking place at a hotel that I own, so they have to give me a table. It's the biggest "do" of the year. Not to be missed.'

'You're very kind, but we're busy—' Justin began.

'I think not,' Carlo interrupted him swiftly. 'I'm sure we have no plans for tomorrow night.'

Understanding what was expected of him, Justin hastily backtracked, and within a short time they were engaged for the next evening.

'I think you've taken leave of your senses,' Justin observed in the car afterwards.

'Oh, yes,' Carlo said quietly. 'That happened a long time ago.'

Della didn't recognise him at first. It was late at night and she was half asleep in front of the television. Through the sleepy haze she heard a man's voice saying, 'Far too much has been made of…sense of proportion—'

Then another man began to talk, and she felt disorientated because the voice was Carlo's but the appearance wasn't. She blinked, forcing herself to focus, and realised that it really was him but, with his shaggy locks cut off, almost unrecognisable.

His boyish looks had owed a lot to the neglect of his hair, she realised. With most of it gone, he seemed like someone else, serious, intense, and learned. She didn't understand a word he was saying, beyond the fact that he was defending a recent discovery against those who would dismiss it. He was fierce and angry, almost contemptuous.

It was strange to see him as never before, and yet to recognise him. This wasn't the young man who'd loved her passionately through the long, hot nights, and laughed with her through the sunny days. This man was stern, controlled, radiating a conviction that the world must take him on his own terms or not at all. Her heart ached as she watched him.

At any moment he would smile, and it would be the smile she loved, that had brightened the world. But suddenly the programme was over, and he hadn't smiled once.

She discovered that she was leaning forward, her whole body tense, shaking. She wanted to reach out and touch him, but he wasn't there. He never really had been there. He would never be there again, and the tears were pouring down her face.

She tried to put him out of her mind and concentrate on the coming award ceremony. She decided to wear the elegant black cocktail dress she'd bought in Italy, and when it was on she knew she looked her best. She'd lost weight in the last few weeks, and had the figure of a girl, which the tight black dress emphasised. Her make-up was skilled and professional. This was going to be her big night.

And she would make the most of it, she decided. For professional triumph was the only satisfaction she would know for the rest of her life.

Her 'date' was her assistant, George Franklin, who had earned tonight almost as much as she had.

'The word on the grapevine is that you've won,' he told her, as they reached their table and he pulled out a chair for her.

'Go on with you,' she chided, trying to not to hope for too much. 'I'll bet we've all been told that.'

He grinned, and she thought how different he looked in a dinner jacket. Normally she saw him only in jeans and old sweaters, but now, shaved and almost elegant, he looked reasonably attractive, carrying his fifty years lightly.

The ceremony began. Factual programmes were dealt with first, and in half an hour the announcer was proclaiming, 'Now the award for the best documentary series. The contenders are—'

He read out five names, and the screen showed five brief extracts from the programmes.

'And the winner is—Della Hadley for *The Past is the Future*.'

She was a popular choice, and the applause swelled as she approached the stage. There she delivered a brief acceptance speech and departed quickly, to more applause. As she went back down the room lights flashed, blinding her, and when she'd blinked and recovered she found herself looking straight at the one person she'd thought never to meet again.

People were pushing past in each direction, but neither of them noticed. The world had stopped, leaving them on an island.

'Congratulations,' he said, seeming to speak from a distance.

'I—thank you.' He didn't say any more, but stood looking at her with something in his eyes that she didn't want to see. It saddened her too much. 'I didn't expect to see you here,' she said, for something to say.

'I was invited at the last minute. You're looking well.'

'So are you,' she said. 'But I wouldn't have recognised you if I hadn't seen you on the box the other night.'

'You saw that?'

'You slaughtered the opposition. I couldn't follow a word, but I understood that much.' She gave an awkward laugh. 'I was right about you. You're a natural on television.'

'Thank you,' he said lamely. After a moment he asked, 'What happened about the series?'

'I'm still doing it, using several different presenters.'

'Will you be going to the same places?'

'Not all of them. I changed some. I've included the wreck of the *Britannic*.'

'You managed to find someone who wasn't chicken, then?'

'Yes, I did.'

Silence.

'I'm glad you're still doing the series,' he said.

'Yes, so am I.'

It was months since their last meeting, and now the air about them seemed to clamour with unspoken thoughts and feelings. But these commonplaces were all that would come.

There was a brief agitation around them as people tried to get past.

'We're in everyone's way,' she said. 'It was nice seeing you again.'

'And you.'

Carlo watched her return to her table, waiting for the moment when she would look back at him. It never came. He saw a middle-aged man rise, put his arm around her and kiss her cheek. So that was her escort, he thought, no doubt chosen for his suitability.

He'd said she was looking well, but the truth was she was looking fantastic: beautiful, glamorous, sexy, every man's dream. After the way she'd claimed to be getting old it was like another rejection hurled at him.

He returned to his own table, where his family were regarding him with curiosity, and Alan Forest with awe.

'You know her?' he asked, wide-eyed.

'We met once briefly.' He was still standing, watching her, willing her to turn and look at him.

'Get her over here—we'll all celebrate together.'

'I'm sure she has her own arrangements,' Carlo said, trying to keep the tension out of his voice.

'Nonsense. We'll have a great time—'

'I don't think we should trouble them,' Evie broke in quickly. 'She's with a party of her own.'

Della was certainly having a night of triumph. People were coming up to congratulate her, kiss her, admire the award. The man with her was regarding her with proprietary pride, and it was clear to Carlo that everyone else saw them as a couple.

As he watched, Della lifted the statuette, so that it glittered in the light, and her crowd of admirers cheered and applauded.

Then she finally turned his way, and for a moment their glances locked. He thought her smile grew broader, her eyes more triumphant, as though she was telling him something.

He understood. She did very well without him. Just as she had always known she would. She had tried to warn him, but in his blind arrogance and stupidity he'd refused to see it.

'I guess you're right,' Alan Forest said, beside him. 'That lady doesn't need us. She's got everything she could ever want in the world.'

'Yes,' Carlo said, almost inaudibly. 'She has.'

He sat down, and after a moment he felt Evie's

hand creep into his and give a sympathetic squeeze.

The next day he went home.

The award was the most prestigious there was, and it set the seal on her career. Congratulations poured in, also offers. Now everyone wanted her.

As well as work, she could occupy herself with Gina's pregnancy, but she soon discovered that she was no longer needed. The Christmas visit to the grandmother had been a success, and it wasn't long before Mrs Burton invited Gina to make her home with her.

'I still want you to be part of the baby's life,' Gina explained to Della. 'But—'

'But you want to be with your own family. Of course you do.'

'I'll never forget what you've done for me.'

Her new home was a hundred miles away, just too far for easy visiting.

On the last day of February Della escorted the girl there herself, and it was a happy occasion. Mrs Burton was a vigorous woman in her sixties, prosperous enough to take on the new responsibility, and eager to do so. She and Della established cordial relations, and there was an open invitation to visit.

It had ended well, but as she returned home Della realised that she was more alone than ever.

She reached the houseboat in the middle of a thunderstorm. Rain poured down in torrents, and it was a relief to get inside. Soon she'd dried off and done her best to get warm, but somehow it didn't work. There was a part of her that remained trapped in a chill desert, and no amount of heating could reach it.

She went to look at the statuette, high on a shelf where it could broadcast her achievement, trying to draw comfort from it. But it only reminded her of that night, and his face, tense and drawn. Something was destroying him, just as it was destroying her.

She wondered if he, like her, had an ache in his heart so intense that it was an actual physical pain that went on and on. It had been there for months and she was beginning to wonder if it would ever fade.

But surely she'd made the right decision?

She listened, almost as though expecting a voice to answer her. But the only sound was the drumming of the rain in a bleak universe.

Reaching into a drawer, she took out the folder of pictures from her time in Naples. There were a hundred stills, plus a disk recorded in a camcorder, taken by a friendly passerby. Since returning she'd rarely allowed herself to look at it, but now she slipped it into the machine.

It was like watching strangers. The man and the woman were totally in love, totally right for each other, rejoicing in that rightness. Nobody watching would have known that her thoughts were far away, planning to leave him. Certainly he hadn't known. There was a defenceless innocence in his manner towards her because he trusted her totally.

And he was wrong, she thought, tears streaming down her face. He shouldn't have trusted her for a moment, because she'd been planning to betray him. He'd never suspected because there wasn't a dishonest bone in his body, and when he found out it had nearly ruined him. Even then he'd wanted her back, and she'd refused because she hadn't one tenth of his courage.

She could hardly bear to look at the blissfully happy young joker before her eyes. He'd gone, replaced by the haggard, distant man she'd seen at the awards. And she had done that to him.

She switched off and sat in the darkness for a long time.

If I go to Naples, he'll know the truth as soon as he sees me. He'll know I can't keep away from him. How can I tell him that, after what happened?

Pride. It mattered, didn't it?

The drumming of the rain seemed to give her the answer. Pride. Emptiness. A lifetime without love. Years of endless, searing misery.

Or the flowering that was there inside her at the thought of seeing him again. It spread, streaming through her veins, taking her over until there was nothing left but joy.

I could tell him that I love him, and that I got it wrong. Maybe there's even a chance we can still find the way. But if not, if it's too late, at least I can tell him that I'm sorry.

* * *

While she waited for the flight to be called she sat down for a coffee, and at once her cellphone went. It was Sol.

'Where are you?' he demanded. 'I just got a text saying you were going away for a few days—'

'I'm going to Naples.'

'To see him?'

'No,' she said quickly. She couldn't bear Sol to know the truth just yet. 'I'm still looking over sites—tying up loose ends. I'll be in touch.'

'Yeah. Right. How long will you be gone?'

'I don't know. I have to go now.'

Della was hardly aware of taking her seat, fastening the belt. She was on edge until the plane rose from the ground, and then there was the relief of knowing that the decision was final.

The flight to Naples was three hours. She began to wonder what she would do, having made no plan of action beyond putting up at the Vallini.

I don't even know where he is. He may not be at Pompeii now, or even be in Naples any more.

She tried not to think that she might arrive too late, closing her eyes, fighting the fear. But the thought took hold of her. Her whole life might be haunted by her failure to find him in time. Then a sudden violent lurch brought her back to the present. She opened her eyes to find everyone looking around in alarm.

'Ladies and gentlemen, we are experiencing a little turbulence. Please fasten your seatbelts…'

She hated this, but comforted herself with the thought that it wasn't far now. It was hard to fasten the belt because another lurch made it fly out of her hand.

You're nearly there now. Concentrate on that thought, and on seeing him again.

She finally managed to fasten the clasp and sat back, taking deep breaths. She could feel that they were going down, so this was nearly over.

But then she heard the screams begin, and she knew that it wasn't nearly over. The worst was just beginning.

'So you're off to Egypt?' Hope asked.

'I thought you said Egypt had been done to death?' observed Ruggiero from further down the table, where the three of them were breakfasting on the terrace of the villa.

'It's just a stop on the way,' Carlo said. 'Then Thailand. Then—I forget.'

'You sound as though it doesn't matter,' Hope said, alarmed. 'But in the past when you started a new job you were always lit up inside. Today—you *shrug*. You do that too often, as though nothing mattered any more.'

'You're being fanciful, Mamma. Of course something matters—my new contract with Mr Forest, which will give me freedom to go anywhere and research anything.'

'And it will keep you away for a long time—which is what you really want, isn't it?' she asked shrewdly.

He almost shrugged again, but stopped himself, conscious of his mother's all-seeing eyes. It was true that he'd seized the chance of an alliance with the man he'd met in England. Alan Forest could fund his research, freeing him to travel anywhere for as long as he pleased. But he reasoned that any ambitious archaeologist would have done the same, whatever Hope might imply.

'You're lucky to be able to run away,' Ruggiero remarked.

'I am not running away,' Carlo said sharply.

'Like hell you're not! You even tried to talk Forest out of staying in the Hotel Vallini.'

'Because there are better hotels in Naples,' Carlo said indifferently.

Ruggiero's answer was to make a sound like a chicken clucking.

'I'm going,' Carlo said.

'But you haven't finished your breakfast,' Hope protested.

'I prefer not to listen to the ravings of this person,' Carlo said coolly, jerking his head in his brother's direction.

'I just like a man who's honest with himself,' Ruggiero observed. 'Running to the other side of the world is the reverse of honest.'

'Now, listen, you two,' Carlo said, in the voice of a man exasperated beyond endurance. 'I am not running away. I'm simply not going to spend the rest of my life brooding. It's over. Finished. Della made her decision and that's that. And the more I think of it, the more I realise that she was right. Life goes on.'

Ruggiero drew in his breath. He might or might not have been going to cluck again. It was impossible to say since the look Carlo turned on him effectively froze his blood.

'I'm off,' Carlo said, draining his cup. 'We should have signed that contract two days ago, but better late than never.'

'And after you've gone, when will I see you again?' Hope wanted to know.

'That's in the lap of the gods.' He kissed her cheek and departed.

'He's really changed,' Hope sighed.

'I'll say!' Ruggiero exclaimed with feeling. 'Another moment and he'd have killed me. You know why this is happening suddenly, don't you? It's because he saw her in England.'

'He never talks about that,' Hope said sadly. 'We wouldn't even know if Evie hadn't told us.'

'After that he thought she'd get in touch with him.'

'He said so?'

'No, but he jumped every time his phone went. It was never her.'

'Why didn't he just call her?'

'Mamma, don't you understand him yet? *She* rejected *him*. Very finally. He won't go back to her and beg.'

'But perhaps she called him when you weren't there.'

'No, she never called him.'

'How can you be sure?'

'Because he's going away,' Ruggiero said.

The sight of Alan Forest gave Carlo a shock. He had one arm in a sling, and a black eye.

'Were you mugged?' Carlo asked.

'No, I was on that plane that crashed at the airport a couple of days ago. I expect you saw it on the news. It was a terrible business. Fifteen people dead, several more expected to die.'

'But when you called me to say there'd be a delay in the contract you didn't mention the crash,' Carlo said. 'You just said something had come up.'

'I was out of my mind on sedatives and I just wanted to sleep. They take very good care of you in the Berrotti Hospital. But I'm fine now.'

'Are you sure?' Carlo asked worriedly.

'Believe me, I was one of the lucky ones. But

the others—there was even someone I knew—by sight, anyway. That TV producer you talked to at the awards ceremony.'

'What?' Carlo's cup clattered into the saucer.

'Della somebody—'

'*She* was in that crash?' Carlo asked in a tense voice.

'I saw them carry her off on a stretcher, and she wasn't moving. She could be dead by now. Hey! What are you—?'

He was talking to empty air. Carlo had fled.

Afterwards he couldn't remember how he got to the hospital. He was functioning on automatic, blotting out the hideous truth. For two days she'd been lying within a few miles of him—alone, perhaps dying. And he hadn't known.

At the hospital he parked the car in a hurry and hurled himself inside.

'Signora Hadley,' he said fiercely to the young woman receptionist. 'Where is she?'

'Are you a relative, *signore*?'

'No, but I—know her very well.'

'I'm afraid we have strict rules—'

'For the love of God, tell me she's alive,' he said hoarsely. 'Just say that. *Say it!*'

'She's alive,' she said, regarding him in alarm. '*Signore*, please—don't force me to call Security.'

'No—' He ran his hand through his hair. 'There's no need. I just want to know how badly hurt she is—she was in the crash.'

She relented, taking pity on his haggard face sufficient to say, 'Yes, she was on the plane, and she was brought here.'

'And she's still alive? You said so, didn't you?'

'Yes, I did. She's alive, although I must warn you— Perhaps you'd better talk to her son.'

'He's here?'

'We sent for him at once. If you go up to the second floor, you should find him.'

He was gone before she'd finished talking. As he ran, the receptionist's words hammered in his head. *'I must warn you—I must warn you—'*

He shut them out. He was afraid.

He saw Sol as soon as he turned into the corridor, standing at the far end, staring out of the window, so that at first he was unaware of Carlo's approach. Even when he looked up he didn't seem to recognise the man hurrying towards him, his face harsh and desperate.

'How is she?' Carlo demanded.

'My God, it's you!'

Carlo took a step towards him. He was closer to losing control than he'd ever been in his life.

'How is she?'

'She's been unconscious since they dragged her off that plane,' Sol declared in a flat voice. 'The doctors talk a lot of guff, but we all know what's going to happen.'

Suddenly his voice shook.

'She's dying, and there's nothing anyone can do.'

CHAPTER ELEVEN

'THAT can't be true,' Carlo said harshly. 'I don't believe it.'

'Do you think I haven't said that to myself?' Sol demanded. 'When I first got here and found her unconscious I thought she'd wake up at any moment, but she didn't. It goes on and on. The longer she's unconscious the worse it is. They had to operate, but she should have come round by now.'

'Where is she?'

'Behind that door. They sent me out while they did something with the machines. You should see all the things she's attached to.'

He closed his eyes for a moment before he went on,

'They say she took a terrible bang on the head.

Even if she does come round we just don't know how she'll be—if she'll recognise anyone, or know who she is—'

Carlo turned away swiftly, lest he betray too much.

'I know the doctors expect her to die at any moment,' Sol continued. 'They don't say so outright, but you can tell from the careful way they phrase things.'

Suddenly he glared at Carlo.

'You took your time getting here, damn you!'

'I came as soon as I heard. That was only half an hour ago.'

'Yeah, like you didn't know she was on her way.' Sol's tone was almost a sneer. 'Why the hell couldn't you leave her alone?'

'What are you talking about?' Carlo demanded harshly. 'I haven't been in touch with her since she left.'

'Don't give me that!' Sol snapped. 'Why was she flying to Naples if not to see you?'

'I don't know.'

'I don't believe you. I phoned her at the airport and she— I don't know— Hell!'

'She told you she was coming to me?'

'No, she denied it. But I knew.'

'What did she say?'

'What does it matter?'

'What did she say, damn you?'

Carlo had slammed his shaking hands down on Sol's shoulders, and for a moment looked as though he might be about to throttle him.

'What did she say?' he repeated hoarsely, releasing Sol.

'I can't remember exactly,' the lad said, moving away carefully. 'Something about tying up loose ends—'

'But that could mean anything,' Carlo said, feeling dizzy. 'It could be work. Was there nothing else?'

'Just that she didn't know how long she'd be away—'

Carlo wanted to shake him. Instead he took a step away. It was safer for them both that way.

He felt torn in many directions. He'd longed for Della to return to him, but not at this cost to her. Sooner than see her hurt he would live lonely all his days.

'I didn't know she was coming,' he growled. 'I only heard today that she was on the plane.'

Sol looked at him, his head on one side in an attitude that implied cynicism. Carlo hated him. Then he noticed that the young man's face was pale and haggard, as if something had finally pierced his armour of selfishness. The hatred faded. They both loved the woman who lay beyond the door, fighting for her life, and for her sake he wouldn't quarrel with her son. No matter what.

'I didn't know she was coming,' he repeated. 'If I had, I'd have been at the airport. Nothing would have kept me away. But since she didn't tell me I think you're wrong, and she came to Naples for another reason.'

Sol shrugged.

They both turned sharply as the door opened and a nurse looked out.

'Signor Hadley—'

'Has she come round?' Sol asked tensely.

'I'm afraid not. But you can come in now.'

Sol hurried back into the room. Carlo tried to follow him, but the nurse stopped him.

'I'm sorry, *signore*, but only one person at a time—'

Carlo looked over her shoulder, feeling stunned. The figure on the bed could have been anyone, but his heart knew her at once.

Then the door closed, shutting him out.

He stayed there for the rest of the day, his gaze fixed on the blank wall, trying not to think. His mind pulled this way and that. She had returned to him and they had a future. She was dying and his own life was over with hers.

Then his thoughts would shut off, just in time to stop him going crazy.

When he could stand it no longer he went and opened the door. At once the nurse came to fend him off.

'I'm sorry. You can't—'

'Let him in.' Sol's voice came from the bed. He muttered as Carlo approached, 'Let him see what he did.'

Now he could see her clearly, and it was a nightmare. Her head was swathed in bandages and her eyes were covered.

'What happened to her?' he whispered.

'Her head was injured and we had to operate,' the nurse said. 'And there's some damage to her eyes. Just how bad it is we don't know yet.'

'That's if she lives,' Sol added with soft fury.

Carlo was looking at the machines, with their flashing lights and occasional clicks, measuring her heart-rate, blood pressure, and a dozen other things—too many to take in. A tube, leading to an oxygen machine, was clamped brutally into her mouth.

There were other attachments—one to a blood transfusion, one to a saline drip, one to a pain-killer—all connected to her by small cables attached to inserts in her flesh—two in her arm, one in her hand, and one, he winced to notice it, directly into her neck.

If they had been alone there were a million things he wanted to say to her, but now he could only stand and watch, helpless.

A buzzer sounded, and the nurse answered urgently, 'Yes—all right. I'm on my way.'

To the others she said, 'I have to leave for a moment. If her condition changes press that bell.'

She hurried out.

'You look done in,' Carlo said. 'Why don't you go and get yourself some coffee?'

Sol shrugged, lacking the energy for an argument, and slipped out.

Carlo sat beside the bed, not taking his eyes from her. He wanted to speak, but his throat ached too much. If only she would move. But she lay as deathly still as if—his appalled mind found the connection—as if she'd been there for two thousand years.

That thought brought her back to him as she'd been on that first day, when she'd danced into his life, turning the world upside down so that everything settled back into a different place. Together they had stood looking at the silent lovers, and now the memory broke his heart.

He leaned as close as he dared, whispering so that his breath touched her cheek.

'Do you remember that day? How they held each other? I knew then that one day we would hold each other like that—did you know it, too? Why were you returning to Naples? Was it for me?

'Where are you now? Have you really started on that road where the light beckons at the other end and your memories of the world are fading? Do you know that I'm behind you, calling you back? How can I make you turn to me?

'Do you know that I love you? Wherever you are, whatever has happened to you, whatever the future holds for us, I love you. If you live, I love you. If you—if you die, I shall love you and only you. You'll always be in my heart. We'll never really lose each other, and one day we'll be together again. I don't know where, or how long it will take, but it can never be over for us.

'Until then, I belong to you as totally as I say you belong to me, as finally as though the words had been said before an altar. Nothing could make me more yours than I am at this moment.'

He moved his fingers gently, so that they were beneath hers.

'They say that hearing outlasts the other senses. Is that true? Can you hear me? If only you could let me know! Can't you squeeze my hand, even slightly?'

But she never moved. It was as though she was dead already.

The door opened and a man in a white coat looked in, surprised at the sight of him.

'The nurse was called away,' Carlo said.

'But I haven't seen you here before. Who are you?'

Carlo rose to his feet.

'I am her husband,' he said.

The darkness was everywhere, but it changed quality all the time: sometimes thick and impenetrable, sometimes shot through with coloured flashes. Mixed with the darkness was the hideous noise.

There had been a blow on her head as the plane smashed into the runway. When she'd become half conscious again she'd found that opening her eyes was searingly painful, and given up the attempt. Dazed, she'd lain, listening to the screams around her, shouts, cries for help.

Someone yelled, 'Get that ambulance here quickly.'

Then another voice said, more quietly, 'This one's dead. Who's next?'

A violent jolt sent pain shrieking through her

body, and the sounds vanished. Then there was only blackness, hot and swirling about her head.

She recovered consciousness, lost it, regained it, lost it again, until she could no longer tell one state from another. The air grew cooler, voices changed, pain faded, everything became blessedly peaceful. But it was the peace of nothing.

The world grew dim, leaving her in isolation through which presences came and went. Ghosts danced around her—Carlo as he'd been in their happy days, reaching out to take her in his arms and lead her to the new life that had beckoned for them, which she had rejected.

She could see Sol—and somehow Gina was there, but she faded, then Sol faded. Only Carlo was left, and he was running away from her. He knew that she'd come to Naples to find him and he didn't want her any more.

She was tired now. All she had to do was walk on, to a place where she could sleep, but suddenly he was there behind her, calling, pleading, demanding that she turn back because he was her husband.

She tried to think how that had happened, but

everything was confusion and at last she knew that it did not matter. He had claimed her, and she was safe.

Sol returned two hours later, looking sheepish.

'I fell asleep in the café,' he said.

'Don't worry about it,' Carlo said. He was feeling in charity with Sol for leaving him alone for so long, even by accident.

'Has there been any change?'

Before Carlo could answer a doctor and nurse came in. After studying the machines the doctor said, 'It's strange how sometimes that happens, very suddenly.'

'What happens?' Carlo asked sharply.

'The vital signs simply start to improve for no apparent reason. It's happening here. Heart-rate, breathing, blood pressure—all better. Good. Let's try disconnecting the breathing machine. If your wife can breathe on her own, that'll be a big step forward.'

Sol looked puzzled at the word 'wife', but after a glance at Carlo's face he said nothing, and both of them stood back while the machine was disconnected.

The tense silence that followed seemed to go on for ever. Then Della's chest heaved, and she was breathing. The nurse smiled, the doctor hissed a soft 'Yes!' and Sol and Carlo thumped each other on the shoulder.

Carlo was the first to stop, turning away and hurrying out of the room, so that nobody should see him weep. He stayed a long time at the window in the corridor, convulsed with silent sobs, trying to bring himself under control.

'Carlo!'

He turned to see his mother, advancing from the far end of the corridor. She opened her arms to him and he went into them willingly.

'What are you doing here?' he asked huskily.

'Signor Forest called the villa, asking about you. When he told us what had happened I knew everything. How is she?'

'She's very, very ill, Mamma. She's just started to breathe unaided, but it's only the start. She's still unconscious, and she may be blind. I've tried talking to her, telling her that I'm here for her. I hoped it might help her fight.'

'You must be patient, my son. This will take time, so I brought you a bag with some clean clothes and shaving things. I expect you'll be here for a while.' She gave him the bag, adding, 'Call home as often as you can. I want to be kept up to date.'

When she had left he called Alan Forest to explain, apologise, and thank him for talking to Hope.

'No need to say more,' Alan told him kindly. 'I got the picture as soon as you dashed off. Good luck. Maybe we'll work together one day.'

He returned to Della's room find the doctor talking,

'It's looking better, but it's too soon to uncross our fingers. As I expect you know, she's already had a heart attack.'

'No, I didn't know,' Carlo said sharply.

'It happened on the first day. It was mild, but in her condition everything is serious.'

It took two more days for Della to be declared out of danger. The staff were still unwilling to let them both be in the room together, so he and Sol reached a working arrangement under which they took it in turns.

As hour followed hour the machines showed that she was growing stronger, and he tried to think ahead. But he hit a brick wall, unable to imagine what the future held.

It seemed to him the most brutal ill luck that he wasn't there when she finally came round. He came in to find Sol rejoicing, while Della had relapsed into unconsciousness.

'What did she say?' Carlo demanded.

'Not much,' Sol told him. 'I held her hand and told her who I was, and she knew me. Her mind's clear.'

'Did you tell her I was here?'

'No. I'm not sure how much she can take in yet. The doctor said not to put pressure on her.'

It was reasonable, but Carlo's disappointment was bitter.

Sol watched Carlo struggling to come to terms with it, and saw what the effort at self-control did to him. A grudging respect tinged his hostility and he said, 'OK, there's something you'd better see. I had to go through her stuff, and I found this in the hand luggage.' He handed Carlo a thick envelope. 'I guess it tells its own story.'

He left the room quickly, giving Carlo no chance to reply.

The envelope contained photographs. Letting them spill onto the bed, Carlo saw his own face a hundred times, either alone or with her. They had all been taken during their first glorious week together, and she had brought them with her, in her hand luggage. Perhaps she had even looked at them during the flight.

She had been coming back to him. Nothing else could account for this.

But his first leap of delight was overtaken by another feeling as he studied the pictures. They showed him to himself in a new light. Here was a man clearly in love, but equally clearly driven by possessiveness. He'd made jokes about being her slave, but his hands had always been holding her tightly, as though fearing to free her to make her own decisions.

How often had he pressed her to do what he wanted? How often had she begged for more time? In the end he'd suffocated her, driving her to flee. It was his fault that she was lying here.

He sat beside her, watching her face, silently pleading with her to wake up and speak to him. Because more than anything in the world he wanted to tell her that he was sorry.

He stayed with Della for the next few hours, talking, praying that she could hear him, but when his stint was over she had still given no sign. At last Sol came in.

'Anything?'

'No.' He pointed to the envelope. 'Thanks.'

'Did it tell you what you wanted to know?'

'It told me a lot more than I wanted to know. I think I even know why she didn't call me before coming out here.'

'Well, the two of you can sort it out next time she wakes up. OK—my turn.'

Carlo went to the door, but he couldn't resist turning for a last hopeful look at Della.

It took all his self-control to stand there, unknown to her, watching her suffer but unable to offer her any comfort. He clenched and unclenched his hands, willing her to awaken while he was still here.

'Sol—'

The voice from the bed was so faint that they had to strain to hear it.

'Sol, are you there?' Della reached out as she spoke, grasping frantically at the air.

'I'm here,' he said quickly, taking her hand and returning to the chair by the bed. 'Just as I was last time.'

'I thought you'd gone.'

'No, I'll be here as long as you want me.'

'I'm just being silly. I'm sorry. I get these funny ideas.'

'What kind of ideas?'

'Just fancies. I imagined—'

Sol looked over his shoulder. Silently Carlo mouthed, *Tell her.*

'There's something I've got to tell you,' Sol said, turning back to Della. 'Carlo's been here. He heard about what happened and he's worried about you.'

Carlo waited for her to smile, to call for him, but instead she was suddenly frantic.

'You haven't let him in here?' she cried in a cracked voice. 'Promise me that you haven't.'

'Mum—'

'You won't let him in here, will you?'

'But I thought you still—'

'Thought I what?'

'You know,' he said, uneasy and embarrassed.

'Still love him?'

'Yeah. That.'

In the doorway Carlo tensed, waiting for her answer. The silence seemed to go on for ever.

'Of course I love him,' Della said softly. 'And I always will. But it's too late. I couldn't bear him to see me like this. You haven't let him in, have you?'

Faced with her mounting agitation Sol had no choice but to say, 'No, I swear I haven't.' He saw Carlo's hands raised in protest and gave him a desperate shrug as if to say, What else could I do?

'He mustn't see me.' Della's voice rose to a cry. 'Promise me—promise me—'

'I promise—Mum, I promise. But I think you're wrong. The guy loves you, for Pete's sake.'

'He loved me as I was then, but he's never seen me like this, and I don't want him to.'

Carlo had recovered enough to mouth, *Makes no difference.*

'Maybe it wouldn't make any difference,' Sol recited obediently.

'That's what he'd say,' Della murmured. 'And he'd mean it, because he's kind and generous, but I couldn't put such a burden on him. It wouldn't be fair.'

'Maybe love isn't fair,' Sol replied, repeating Carlo's silent message.

'It isn't. If it were—if love was fair—I could find a way not to love him so much. I've tried not to—I thought I could forget—be strong—but he's always there. No, it's not fair—'

Sol looked up again, expecting some direction, but Carlo was leaning against the wall, his face distorted, his hands hanging helplessly by his sides. It was as if Della last words had knocked the strength out of him.

'Perhaps you don't really want him to go?' Sol suggested, dragging some inspiration from inside himself.

'That's very clever of you, darling. It's true, I don't want to lose what we had, but I can only keep it now by letting it go and remembering.'

'Let me bring him here,' Sol urged.

'No—no! You mustn't do that. Sol, I'm trusting you. I can trust you, can't I? You wouldn't deceive me about this?'

'No, I— Of course you can trust me, Mum.'

'Don't you see why I could never let Carlo see me this way? I want him to remember me as I was the last time he saw me.' Her lips curved in a sudden smile. 'It was the awards night. I was dressed to kill and I know I looked good—you saw the tape—my best ever. He was there, and he saw me. I'll never look as good as that again. But it doesn't matter because he'll never know. He'll remember me as I was that night, and that's what I want.'

'But think of all your life—' Sol began to argue.

'I can manage if I know he's all right. What I couldn't bear is to tie him down when he should be flying.'

'Flying?'

'On the first day he told me about his ambitions, how he wanted to do something that could send him soaring. No nine-to-five job or collar and tie for him. That's what I want for him, too. I couldn't bear to be the one to take it away.'

'Can you really live on memories for ever?' Sol asked.

Again she smiled—an incredible smile, breathtaking in its happiness.

'I have the very best memories,' she said softly.

After that there was silence. When Sol looked at the door again, Carlo had gone.

CHAPTER TWELVE

DOWN the side of the hospital ran a narrow street, lined with small shops and cafés, some with outside tables. At one of them sat Carlo, drinking coffee, staring fiercely at the floor.

'Well, look who's here!'

He looked up to see Ruggiero pulling out chairs for Hope and himself. His brother called the waiter and ordered *prosecco* all round.

'Is that her window up there?' Hope asked, pointing to the hospital.

'That's right. The third one along. How did you know I was here?'

'We've been spying on you, of course,' Ruggiero said. 'What else?'

'Why aren't you with her?' Hope demanded. 'That's where you belong.'

'So I thought,' he said heavily. 'But I was

wrong. She doesn't want to see me. The mere idea upsets her.'

'Because she no longer loves you?'

'Because she thinks I won't want her now she's injured.'

'Perhaps she's right?' Hope said carefully. 'She'll be a heavy responsibility.'

His eyes flashed. 'Do you think I'm afraid of that?'

Hope looked at him thoughtfully for a moment.

'No,' she said at last. 'I don't think so.'

'But *she* does.'

'Then you must convince her otherwise. It should be easy, since she loves you so much. After all, she came back to find you.'

'Yes, I think she did. But the crash has changed everything—not for me, but for her.

'Nonsense. She still wants you. Nothing has changed,' Hope said robustly. 'Your mother says so, and your mother is always right.'

He gave a faint smile, but looked at her curiously. 'At one time you were against her.'

'In those days I was a stupid woman. I didn't understand her, but most of all I didn't understand you. I see more clearly now.'

She saw Carlo glance up at the window, to where a young man stood, signalling to him.

'Sol,' he explained.

'You two have become friends?' Ruggiero demanded sceptically.

'Not quite that, but we're managing to work together. He's not so bad.' He rose and kissed her cheek. 'Thank you, Mamma, for everything.'

'Give Della my love.'

He found Sol in the corridor, agitated.

'Now we're in the soup,' he said. 'Why did you tell that doctor that you were her husband?'

'What's happened?'

'He told her about it, didn't he? Only she didn't know, and she asked me a lot of questions, and now she's all worked up and I don't know what to do.'

'But I do. Stay here, and don't come in.'

He found the doctor beside Della's bed, trying to soothe her.

'Please leave,' Carlo said.

'*Signore*, I don't know who you are, but I cannot allow—'

'I am her husband and I tell you to leave.'

The doctor departed quickly. There was something about Carlo that he didn't want to argue with.

Carlo paid him no attention. He'd heard Della's horrified gasp and he dropped down beside the bed, taking her hands in his and kissing them.

'No, don't struggle,' he said. 'Or we'll both get tangled up in your machines. Hush, be still.'

Either his voice or the feel of his hands seemed to get through to her, and at last she lay quiet.

'Is it you?' she whispered.

'Who else should it be? Della, my love—my love—'

She grew still, knowing she should fight this, but also knowing that she had no strength left to fight. She had come to the end, and he was there, waiting for her.

Then she felt the sensation that had haunted her dreams: the gentle pressure of his head against her, so that her hands moved instinctively to enfold and caress him possessively. It wasn't what she'd meant to do, but the choice was no longer hers. As her fingers clasped him she felt him move a little closer, as though seeking a long-lost refuge.

'Do you think you could keep me away?' he

whispered. 'You never could and you never will. Don't try to leave me again, my darling. I couldn't bear it.'

'But look at me,' she said huskily. 'I'm crippled and half blind—or maybe completely blind—'

He raised his head, looking down at what he could see of her wan face, half covered in bandages.

'It doesn't matter,' he said, 'as long as we love each other.'

'But—'

'No.' He laid a gentle finger over her lips. 'No more words. They only get in the way.'

This time they held each other in silence for a long time.

'You told them you were my husband?' she said after a while.

'Yes, because I am. I won't let anyone deny me—not even you. Only tell me this. Why did you come back?'

'To find you. I should never have gone away, and I wanted to tell you that. Even if you didn't want me any more—'

'Hush,' he said, silencing her mouth tenderly

with his own. 'I could never stop wanting you. If you knew how hard I've hoped that you came back for me. When I saw the pictures I dared to let myself believe, but I needed to hear you say it.'

'Even now that I'm like this?'

'I see no difference in you,' he said simply. 'Except that you are hurt, and need me at last.'

Before such total commitment there was nothing for her to say. She began to weep, the tears pouring out from under the bandages until he kissed them away.

From then they had to be patient as Della progressed by slow inches. Painful life returned to her leg, the bandages were removed from her head, although not from her eyes, and her hair began to grow again.

'It isn't grey, is it?' she asked Carlo anxiously.

'No, it's not grey,' he said, laughing. 'It's fair and soft, in little tight curls, like a shorn lamb. You'll start a new fashion.'

'I can't bear not knowing what I look like. How long before they remove these bandages?'

'Be patient until— Hey what are you doing?'

He moved to stop her, but Della was too fast, taking the edge of the bandage, lifting it just a little, then dropping it at once.

'What is it?' he asked, full of dread. 'My darling, don't panic—'

'I think I can see,' she said breathlessly. 'My right eye is fuzzy, but I can make out shapes and colours. *I'm going to see.*'

They flung themselves into each other's arms and stayed that way for a while, unable to speak. Then Della, inspired by sudden determination, raised her hands to her head. But Carlo caught them.

'No, *cara*. We'll ask the doctor before we do anything rash.'

'But he'll just tell me to be patient, and I'm tired of that.'

'One step at a time.'

'I'm sorry,' she said grumpily, resting her head on his shoulder. 'But I'm fed up. I'm fed up with being here, with not being able to move properly, with not knowing what's happening. *I'm fed up.*'

He laughed, caressing her.

'I can see you're going to be a handful to look after.'

'You won't have to look after me.'

'Yes, I will. As soon as you can leave here I'm taking you home, to nurse you until you're well enough for us to be married.'

A noise outside made them pull apart. It was the doctor.

'I can see,' Della told him at once. 'Just out of one eye, but I can.'

'In that case, let's have a look.'

They held their breath as he removed the bandages. Della blinked rapidly.

'I've got the right one back,' she said joyfully. 'It's getting clearer all the time.'

'And the left?'

'Nothing.'

'Well, we may be able to do something about that later.'

'Just one eye makes all the difference,' she said fervently.

The doctor asked some more questions, and went away looking pleased.

'It's so good to see you again,' she said,

meaning it. 'I thought I never would.' She blinked again. 'It's getting better all the time. I'll be able to work again.'

'Will you wait until the rest of you has recovered?' He was almost tearing his hair.

'Sorry. I can't help it.'

Seeing that she was on a high of delight, he gave up trying to calm her down and joined in her pleasure. His own heart was rejoicing at her happiness, content to forget the future in the first good news they'd had.

Sol arrived, already exulting.

'I met the doctor on the way in,' he said, producing a bottle of champagne, 'and turned back to get this.'

They drank it out of paper cups, toasting each other cheerfully, until Della said, 'Darling, it's wonderful that you're here, but now I'm so much better I want you to go home. Your exams must be coming up soon.'

He nodded. 'And I really must pass them this time,' he said. 'I've got to get a job and start sending Gina money. Her grandmother says I can visit them as soon as the baby's born.'

'You've been in touch?'

'I found Mrs Burton's phone number in your things, and—well, I thought I should do something. It's my kid, after all.'

'Good for you,' Carlo said.

Next day he drove Sol to the airport. Now on easy terms, they had a coffee while they waited for the flight to be called.

'You know,' Sol said, considering, 'you didn't handle it very cleverly last year.'

'Handle what?' Carlo asked.

'Everything. "Marry me now or it's all off." I ask you!'

'She told you about that?' Carlo asked, horrified.

'No, of course not. She told Jackie, her secretary. They're friendly.'

'And Jackie told you?'

'Nah, I was eavesdropping.'

'Why didn't I think of that?'

'Dunno. Usually you assume the worst of me on instinct—'

'Maybe I don't any more. A lot of things have changed. Go on with what you were saying.'

'Mum's as stubborn as a mule. Give her an ultimatum and she's off in the other direction. You should have played along with her.'

'Settled for an affair because she thought I was too young?'

'That was just talk,' Sol declared, with the wisdom of twenty-one. 'Once she'd got used to living with you she'd have seen that you were right. When the time came to leave she wouldn't have been able to. You'd have been married by now.'

The truth of this was so blindingly obvious that Carlo nearly burst out laughing.

'If anyone had told me that I'd be sitting here taking advice from you,' he murmured, 'I'd never have believed them.'

At the gate he clapped Sol on the shoulder.

'Good luck,' he said. 'See you again soon.'

It was Hope who took over the arrangements for the day Della left hospital. When she heard that Carlo planned to take her to his apartment she vetoed the idea without hesitation.

'That place is on the third floor, and quite unsuitable,' she declared.

'There is an elevator, Mamma,' Carlo observed,

but he spoke mildly, for he could see where Hope was leading, and it pleased him.

'No arguments,' she said with finality. 'I have decided. She's coming home with us. It's all settled.'

Della had a demonstration of exactly what it meant to be Hope Rinucci when it came to persuading the hospital to let her go early. At first the doctor was dubious, but Hope swept him off to the villa, showed him the ground-floor rooms that were being prepared for the invalid, and emphasised that there would always be people there to care for her.

'She will never be alone in the house,' Hope insisted. 'Not for one moment, even when the nurse has left—for of course I will hire a nurse at the start.'

Della began to see how alike Carlo and his mother were. The same quiet forcefulness was present in both of them.

On the day she left hospital the doctor took Carlo aside.

'There are things you need to know, *signore*. She's better, but her health has been seriously impaired, and it always will be. She had a heart attack immediately after the crash, and she'll always be vulnerable to another one. If you're thinking of having children—'

'No,' Carlo said at once. 'I won't do anything that means the smallest risk for her.'

'Good. Hopefully that will prolong her life.'

'But not by much,' Carlo said quietly. 'Is that what you mean?'

'With the greatest care she could have another twenty years. But she'll always be frail, and it might be less.'

'Whatever it is, it'll still be more than I feared.'

'I'm glad you're a realist, *signore*. You're going to need to be.'

Carlo travelled in the ambulance with her. At the villa she was greeted by Toni and Hope, Ruggiero, Primo and Olympia, and with flowers and messages of goodwill from the others of her new family who could not be there.

They had prepared a home for her, with a room for herself—so well equipped that she might still have been in hospital—a room next door for the nurse, and one nearby for Carlo.

At first they left her alone, knowing that she would need rest more than anything, and she slept for two days before waking to feel better than for a long time.

Now Carlo was with her all the time, even when the nurse was tending her. He watched everything the nurse did, and learned. It was he who got her back on her feet and held her as she struggled to walk again. From a sedentary life she progressed to a walking stick, first clasping him with her free hand, then without him.

'You're improving fast,' he told her. 'At this rate we can start planning the wedding.'

She sat down, gasping slightly from the effort she had made.

'Are you really sure you still want to go ahead?' she asked. 'It's such an undertaking—'

'You mean you don't think you can face a lifetime with me?' he asked wickedly.

'You know what I mean. The cost to you will be much greater now.'

'I can't believe that we're still arguing about this. We settled it long ago. In my heart you are already my wife. Now you will become my wife in the eyes of the world. That's it. Final. End of subject.'

'You don't give me any choice?'

'It's taken you so long to realise that?' he asked, with a touch of his old humour.

'But one day—' Della stopped, silenced by the look he gave her.

She'd been going to say that she wouldn't tie him down. He could divorce her whenever he liked.

'No,' he said firmly, following her meaning as if by telepathy. 'Never say that. *Never!*' He kissed her, then spoke more gently.

'It would be treating me like a boy, one who can't make his own decisions, and we've been down that path before. When we marry it must be for real—and for ever.'

'But I can't give you children,' she reminded him.

'Then we must love each other all the more.'

They spent many evenings on the terrace, looking out at the night, wrapped in each other's arms, talking endlessly, discovering each other's minds. She began to realise how little they had talked in the old days, when their fierce passion had left no time for talk. Now he sometimes seemed afraid to touch her for fear of doing harm.

'I'm not breakable,' she told him once, when he had broken off a kiss by sheer will-power. 'We could go into my room and—'

To calm his nerves he took refuge in clowning. 'Make love before our wedding night?' he asked, in mock horror. 'I'm shocked. Shocked!'

'Well, perhaps it's best that you know the truth about me,' she said, matching his mood.

He seized her wandering hand and spoke in a shaking voice.

'Will you stop, please? How much self-control do you think I have?'

'I'm having fun finding out.'

He gave her a hunted look that made her burst out laughing. He joined her, while still gripping her hand out of sheer self-preservation. They made so much noise that Hope came out to see what the commotion was. But beneath the laughter Della saw the seriousness of the man who would never risk her safety, whatever it cost him. And it *did* cost him, she knew. There were evenings when he parted from her abruptly, lest his strength of will collapse, for his desire for her was as great as ever. She loved him for that, too. But most of all she loved him for what she discovered in his mind, in the long talks they had in the semi-darkness.

Now she could tell him about the path she'd travelled as she lay, unconscious, in hospital.

'Everything was scary, dark and confusing. But then I heard you talking to me, telling me that everything would be all right because you were my husband, and you'd look after me.'

'So why did you try to keep me away when you woke up?'

'Because when I came back to reality everything changed. I knew it had been a wonderful dream, and that I had to be sensible.'

'Being sensible has always been our curse,' he observed. 'It's time you stopped that bad habit.'

'I promise never to be sensible again.'

Sometimes she stared anxiously into the mirror, worried that her ordeal might have aged her faster. Her face was thinner, and there were scars around her left eye, which the nurse assured her would fade to thin lines. But to her relief there was no sign of premature grey hair.

'Not like me,' Carlo told her one day. 'Look.'

Incredibly, the first signs of grey had started to appear at the side of his head. She examined them, wondering if suffering had done this to him.

'You'll have to treat me carefully now I'm getting decrepit,' he told her mischievously.

'Don't let him fool you, daughter,' Toni said. 'The Rinuccis always go grey early. It's just a family trait.'

'Spoilsport.' Carlo grinned. 'I was going to make the most of it.'

Toni winked at Della. 'When your name's Rinucci it'll happen to you, too.'

'I didn't think it worked like that,' she said, chuckling.

'You don't believe me? Try being married to this one, and it'll put ten years on you.'

Everyone laughed, and Della felt the world become a brighter place—partly, she thought, because Toni had called her daughter.

Gradually she saw that her looks had changed, but not in the way she'd feared. Her hair, which had merely curved gracefully before, now decided to curl, so that it was easier to wear it much shorter.

'You look like a pretty little elf,' Sol informed her.

'Cheek.'

'No, it's nice.'

And Carlo thought so, too.

Sol was visiting, armed with photos of his newly-born son. He'd gained his degree—not brilliantly, but well enough to escape censure—and had a job lined up for when he returned to England.

Hope was thrilled with the child.

'Our first great-grandson,' she said.

'But, Mamma,' Carlo began to protest, 'he's not— I mean—'

'Are you saying that Della isn't one of us?' Hope demanded.

'Yes, she is. But—'

'Then this baby is also one of us,' Hope said firmly, thus settling the matter for all time.

When Della was well enough to move around almost normally Carlo vanished one day, and returned in the evening with the news that he had taken a job in a local museum. He explained that he would only need to go in on three days a week, which would give him time for his own projects at home, but it was still the kind of conventional employment that he would once have spurned, and Della and Hope were both loud in their dismay.

'What are you thinking of?' Hope asked him when they were alone.

'Money,' he said simply. 'I haven't worked for months and my cash is running out.'

'You've been giving us too much—we can take less—'

'I know that having Della here is expensive, and I won't let that expense fall on you.'

'As though Poppa and I minded—'

'But I mind,' he said, in the quiet, firm voice that was usual with him these days. 'I'm taking this job.'

'For how long?'

He shrugged cheerfully.

'But what about expeditions?'

'I can't risk leaving Della. When she's stronger we might manage some short trips together, but we'll see how it works out.'

Hope said no more. She saw this dazzling son of hers, the most talented, the most brilliant, giving up his chance of an outstanding future. And yet he was happy. Because he'd found something that meant more to him.

At one time she would have blamed Della, but she knew better now.

It was Della herself who brought up the subject, finding Hope alone that evening.

'You must hate me,' she said slowly.

Hope spoke gently. 'I have no reason to hate you. Never think that.'

'You didn't want me to marry him, and you have even more reason now. I'm tying him down, taking up his time when he should be working at his career.'

'Once I would have thought so, too. But now I know that what he's doing is more valuable to him than any career. Before, everything was easy for him—too easy. Then he had to fight for you, and it made a man of him. Don't try to stop him. Take what he offers. Because in doing that you'll be giving him the kind of love that he most needs.'

* * *

On the night before the wedding Hope found Carlo sitting alone under a lamp in the garden.

'What are you reading, my son?' She took the book from his hands. 'English poetry? You?'

'The sonnets of Elizabeth Barrett Browning,' he said, showing her the one that had held his attention. 'I found them through Della.'

'"*How do I love thee?*"' Hope read. '"*Let me count the ways.*"'

'Look at the last line,' Carlo said. 'I've read it so often—' He whispered the words. '"*And if God choose, I shall but love thee better after death.*"'

'Do you think of that very much?' Hope asked, sitting beside him.

'All the time. Twenty years, if we're very lucky. Perhaps fifteen—or less.'

'And then you'll be left alone, with no children and nothing but memories,' Hope said sadly. 'But at least you'll still be young enough to—well—'

'No,' he said at once. 'I won't marry again.'

'My dear boy, you can't know that now.'

'Yes, I can,' he said slowly. 'You'd be amazed at how far and how well I can see ahead. It's as though a mist has cleared, and I can follow the road to the end. I see it all, and I know where I'm going.'

She didn't want to ask the next question, but she needed to know the answer.

'And when you get there? How will you bear it without her?'

'But I won't be without her,' he said quietly. 'She'll always be with me, still loving me, as I'll always love her. Don't worry about me, Mamma. She'll never really leave me.'

His eyes were shining, and she had to look away. The next moment his arm was about her shoulder and he was hugging her.

'Hey, come on,' he said in a rallying voice. 'Don't cry. Everything's all right. Tomorrow's my wedding day. I'm marrying the woman I love, and I'm the happiest man in the world.'

Next day, the women in the family gathered to adorn Della in her ivory lace wedding gown, then to escort her to the main room, where the rest of the family was waiting. Only Carlo and Ruggiero were missing, having gone ahead to the church.

Sol was there to give her away. As he helped

her out of the car she threw away her stick, not needing it now. Waiting for her at the altar was the man who valued her higher than anything else in life.

Sol smiled and offered his arm. She took it, and together they made their way down the aisle to Carlo. As she grew closer she could make out his expression of expectant joy.

Her heart began to speak to him in silent words.

I love you because from the first moment you accepted me wholeheartedly, asking for nothing except that I should be yours, and by valuing me you showed me how to value myself.

I love you because you taught me how to feel love, when I thought I'd never know.

I love you because you showed me that a man's heart can be deeper and more powerful than I had dreamed possible. And then you gave that heart to me, renewing my life, for however long that life may be.

'And, if God choose, I shall but love thee better after death.'

MILLS & BOON PUBLISH EIGHT LARGE PRINT TITLES A MONTH. THESE ARE THE EIGHT TITLES FOR DECEMBER 2007.

———— ❧ ————

TAKEN: THE SPANIARD'S VIRGIN
Lucy Monroe

THE PETRAKOS BRIDE
Lynne Graham

THE BRAZILIAN BOSS'S INNOCENT MISTRESS
Sarah Morgan

FOR THE SHEIKH'S PLEASURE
Annie West

THE ITALIAN'S WIFE BY SUNSET
Lucy Gordon

REUNITED: MARRIAGE IN A MILLION
Liz Fielding

HIS MIRACLE BRIDE
Marion Lennox

BREAK UP TO MAKE UP
Fiona Harper

 MILLS & BOON®
Pure reading pleasure

1107 R

MILLS & BOON PUBLISH EIGHT LARGE PRINT TITLES A MONTH. THESE ARE THE EIGHT TITLES FOR JANUARY 2008.

———————— ❧ ————————

BLACKMAILED INTO THE ITALIAN'S BED
Miranda Lee

THE GREEK TYCOON'S PREGNANT WIFE
Anne Mather

INNOCENT ON HER WEDDING NIGHT
Sara Craven

THE SPANISH DUKE'S VIRGIN BRIDE
Chantelle Shaw

PROMOTED: NANNY TO WIFE
Margaret Way

NEEDED: HER MR RIGHT
Barbara Hannay

OUTBACK BOSS, CITY BRIDE
Jessica Hart

THE BRIDAL CONTRACT
Susan Fox

 MILLS & BOON®
Pure reading pleasure

1207 Rom LP